MONTANA

*Welcome to Big Sky Country! Where spirited
men and women discover love on the range.*

THE TENACITY SOCIAL CLUB

In rough-and-tumble Tenacity, it seems everyone
already knows everyone else—*and* their
business. Finding someone new to date can
be a struggle. But what if your perfect match is
already written in the stars? Pull up a barstool
and open your heart, because you never know
who you might meet at the Tenacity Social Club!

Jenna Lattimore is a new mom and a widow
besides. She's devoted to her baby girl, Robbie,
and convinced she'll never love again—or at least,
not for a very long time. Handsome rancher Diego
Sanchez claims he's not the right guy for her. Yet
his actions speak louder than his words, and in his
strong, protective arms, Jenna finds unexpected
comfort...and just a little bit of hope.

Dear Reader,

Cowboy Diego Sanchez is known around Tenacity,
Montana, for being unwilling to commit to a serious
relationship. He *has* his reasons. But when he finds
himself snowbound overnight with a struggling widowed
mom and her adorable baby, everything changes.

Jenna Lattimore is so drawn to the handsome, helpful
cowboy who tends to her baby daughter with such care
and tenderness that she can almost see him beside her
for life. But Jenna has already lost so much and knows
better than to believe there's such a thing as forever...

Luckily for Diego and Jenna, the Sanchez family—
including beloved Uncle Stanley and his ninetysomething
psychic bride, Winona Cobbs—is around to share a few
lessons about love. I hope you enjoy *The Maverick's
Promise*!

Warm Regards,

Melissa Senate

THE MAVERICK'S PROMISE

MELISSA SENATE

Harlequin

MONTANA MAVERICKS

Special thanks and acknowledgment are given to
Melissa Senate for her contribution to the
Montana Mavericks: The Tenacity Social Club miniseries.

Harlequin®
MONTANA
MAVERICKS

Recycling programs
for this product may
not exist in your area.

ISBN-13: 978-1-335-14318-1

The Maverick's Promise

Harlequin Enterprises ULC
22 Adelaide St. West, 41st Floor
Toronto, Ontario M5H 4E3, Canada
www.Harlequin.com

Printed in Lithuania

MIX
Paper | Supporting
responsible forestry
FSC® C021394

Melissa Senate has written many novels for Harlequin and other publishers, including her debut, *See Jane Date*, which was made into a TV movie. She also wrote seven books for Harlequin Special Edition under the pen name Meg Maxwell. Her novels have been published in over twenty-five countries. Melissa lives on the coast of Maine with her son; their rescue shepherd mix, Flash; and a lap cat named Cleo. For more information, please visit her website, melissasenate.com.

Books by Melissa Senate

Montana Mavericks: The Anniversary Gift

A Lullaby for the Maverick

Montana Mavericks: The Tenacity Social Club

The Maverick's Promise

Harlequin Special Edition

Dawson Family Ranch

The Long-Awaited Christmas Wish
Wyoming Cinderella
Wyoming Matchmaker
His Baby No Matter What
Heir to the Ranch
Santa's Twin Surprise
The Cowboy's Mistaken Identity
Seven Birthday Wishes
Snowbound with a Baby
Triplets Under the Tree
The Rancher Hits the Road
The Cowboy's Christmas Redemption

Visit the Author Profile page
at Harlequin.com for more titles.

Chapter One

"Which Sanchez will be the next to say 'I do'?"

Don't look at me, Diego Sanchez was thinking as his great-uncle Stanley—eightysomething years old and a newlywed himself—asked the group.

The entire family was sitting around a bunch of tables put together in the Tenacity Social Club. Diego's sister Marisa—the youngest of the five siblings—had gotten married today. When the reception had wound down at 10:00 p.m., the Sanchezes were still in celebration mode and had moved the party there. Even Diego, hardly a romantic, had gotten a little choked up at the ceremony at the Goodness & Mercy Nondenominational Church. And watching Marisa and her new husband, Dawson John, slow dance at the reception at the Tenacity Inn, gazing into each other's eyes with such love, had Diego nodding. If you *were* going to get married, it should look like that.

At thirty-three, Diego had long stopped believing in all that for himself. But his family was everything to him, and Marisa's happiness really touched him.

"Nina? Maybe Luca? How about Diego?" Stanley asked with a smile as he wiggled his bushy gray eyebrows and looked across the table at his great-nieces and -nephews.

"I think we can safely say that Julian is next," Diego said, popping a chili-topped nacho into his mouth from the platter in the center of the table. Julian was the eldest of the siblings and very seriously involved. Diego hadn't seen *that* coming, especially since Julian's love, Ruby McKinley, who was sitting beside him, was a single mother with young children. His brother, a father figure? To a four-year-old and a baby? Diego had seen with his own eyes how much Julian loved Ruby and the kids. His brother had become a true family man—and very recently had become the first of the Tenacity Sanchezes to buy land for a ranch of his own. People could surprise you—no one knew that better than Diego.

"Obviously," Stanley said. "I'm just so happy—for myself, for Julian, for Marisa—that I want every one of my great-nieces and -nephews to find their forever love." His dark eyes misting, he put his arm around his bride, ninetysomething-year-old Winona Cobbs-Sanchez.

Darn it. Even Diego might get teary. Stanley and Winona had been *through* it. Last summer, the family had gathered to watch the elderly lovebirds get married. But Winona hadn't shown up. No one had been sure if she'd gotten cold feet or if something had happened—and man, had something happened. She'd been injured and was suffering from amnesia when a psychopath kidnapped her and convinced Winona—for months—that she was his wife—despite her notorious psychic gifts. But thanks to Stanley's determination, he'd found her when no one else could. The power of love, his great-uncle had insisted. The two had finally married to much celebration.

Winona was now staring hard at Diego, her blue eyes boring into him. Chills—in both a good way and a scary way—skittered up his spine. Winona really was psychic. Diego had never believed much in *that* either, but his new great-aunt's gifts could not be denied. She *knew* things. *What* she knew was a secret, though, because she never said much. What she did say was usually so cryptic that no one could understand what she meant—until her pronouncements came true weeks or months later.

"Diego's the second oldest, so I say *he's* next," his sister Nina said with a grin as she pushed her long dark hair behind her shoulders. "Then again, he's not even dating anyone right now, so maybe not."

"Yeah, that part—the maybe not," Diego half mumbled. "Anyone up for old-school pinball?" he asked, desperately hoping to change the subject as he looked around the club for escape from the conversation. The place doubled as a teen hangout during the day—with the alcohol under lock and key until after 7pm.

"I wouldn't count him out," Julian said, not taking the hint as he scooped nachos on his plate. "When love comes along, that's that." He looked at his girlfriend, who leaned over with puckered lips. Julian and Ruby kissed, then fed each other nachos with their arms entwined.

Love won't be coming my way, Diego wanted to say. *Because I'll block it like I always do.* He kept that thought to himself.

He'd been down that treacherous road, he thought, the old flicker of bitterness burning in his gut. He'd gotten hurt bad when he was twenty-six and all these years later, he wasn't over it. He dated, but when the relationship never got to exclusivity, let alone a proposal, a diamond ring and talk of forever and kids, the woman invariably got tired of waiting and said goodbye. Nina, who'd fixed him up a time or two, would shake her head and tell him that someday, someone was going to steal his heart no matter how good he was at dodging his feelings.

Honestly, Diego hoped so. If his brother and sister were right about love, he supposed it would be that powerful. He might be prickly on the subject, but he certainly didn't want to *die* alone. At the same time, he couldn't imagine feeling so strongly about anyone to the point that he'd propose.

Also your fault, Nina had insisted. *You keep all your dates and girlfriends at a football field distance.*

He supposed he did. But anytime he thought about the future, he could hear his ex, whom he'd loved, telling him she was ending things. *You'll never be more than just a cowboy on some middling ranch. You'll never own your own place. And that's where the money is. Sorry, Diego, you're a good guy and hot as hell, but I've got dreams.*

Dagger to the heart. Owning his own ranch had never been *his* dream. Maybe that was why instead of Caroline's words lighting a fire in him, instead of trying to prove her wrong, something in him had deflated with what had felt like truth. Even if he wanted his own ranch, all it demanded financially just wasn't in the cards. His parents had been renting their house, a good-sized cabin, really, on the big ranch where his dad had worked as a hand for decades—and still did. Diego worked right beside his father as a cowboy. It had been more important over the years for Diego to help support his family, something he'd been doing since he was a teenager. He'd managed to save up some money and could *probably* buy a small fixer-upper ranch, but it was either land or livestock, livestock or equipment.

So yes, Diego had lived up to his ex's assessment. And he figured any woman would feel the same way. He didn't exactly have much to offer. Caroline had married a businessman in a nearby town so at least he didn't have to see her around Tenacity. Reminding him that he hadn't been good enough—and still wasn't at thirty-three.

So no, he definitely wasn't next to say "I do."

"I'd never count out Diego," Stanley said, reaching across the table to pat his great-nephew's hand. The pride on his great-uncle's face scratched at Diego's heart. He didn't like to let people down but he was who he was.

Diego tipped his cowboy hat at *Tio* Stanley. He might be in a suit for the wedding, but he rarely went anywhere without a cowboy hat, and tonight he wore his one Stetson, a gift from his parents when he'd graduated from high school. He had on his good cowboy boots for the occasion too.

"Winona, *you* tell us who's next," Nina said. Her voice was light, but Diego could see the wistfulness on his sister's face. Same look she'd had during Marisa and Dawson's wedding ceremony earlier. Nina was twenty-nine and had had romantic relationships, but had never settled down herself.

"The answer is out there," Winona said calmly.

Nina tilted her head. "Out there?"

Diego watched his sister bite her lip. She seemed to be lost in thought about something.

Or someone.

"You know," Nina said, spending a good twenty seconds heaping a bunch of nachos on her plate. "I, um, I've been thinking about Barrett Deroy lately. Just wondering about why he left town so suddenly."

Ah. Of course. Barrett Deroy. Her first love. Her childhood love. He and his family had left Tenacity under mysterious circumstances when he was sixteen. Poof, gone, no forwarding address, no contact. Diego had a feeling that no man would ever come close to meaning to Nina what Barrett had.

"I mean, it's been fifteen years," Nina added, biting her lip again. "I just have so many questions, you know?" She glanced at Stanley. "Maybe you could look into it?" she asked the amateur detective. "To find out more about what happened all those years ago to make the family leave. The 'incident.'"

Diego wondered about that. The incident? He couldn't remember why the Deroys had packed up and left so suddenly. But he could tell by Nina's expression that she wasn't up for questions. Just answers.

"The Deroys don't seem to be on social media at all," Nina added.

Which meant she'd tried to find them—and Barrett.

"I've got you, *mi gran sobrina*," Stanley said with a warm smile. "I'm up for the challenge."

Winona was now staring at Nina. Diego much preferred that to those shrewd blue eyes on him. "The answer is closer than you think," the elderly psychic said, but her attention turned to the bar.

Diego glanced over. Winona didn't often turn her head, so he was curious. There weren't many people here this late, so the long wooden bar with a bunch of stools was almost empty. Winona seemed to be looking at the expanse of wood with initials carved into it. Couples tradition here in Tenacity. His ex had liked fancier places so they'd never come here together—their initials were not among the hundreds covering the bartop.

Diego was about to turn his attention back to the table when he saw a gorgeous woman who'd just come in approach the bar. She was wearing a big pink parka, her cheeks a bit reddened from the cold. Even a few seconds out in the frigid February cold was too much. She pulled down her hood to display long silky red hair. When she turned slightly, he realized she was holding a baby. The tiny human was encased in a pale yellow snowsuit with some kind of animal ears.

Figured. The first woman to turn his head in months had a baby. And was probably married. Just as well. He wasn't looking for anything anyway. At his age, the women he dated were ready to settle down. He might not want to die alone but at this rate he'd be ready for a relationship when he was Stanley's age. At least he knew a shot at love would be possible then.

Still, he couldn't stop watching the woman. She seemed…stressed, which was evident in her body language. Even under that parka he could see she was coiled tight. Her beautiful face was etched with something like worry but not quite that. He couldn't put his finger on it. She was upset, though. He didn't recall ever seeing her before. Maybe she was new in town. Then again, Diego worked hard, hung with his family at home over going out in town, so it was possible that he'd just never run into her.

He watched the bartender, who Diego didn't know, come around the long bar toward the woman. She carefully handed him the baby. Her husband?

Lucky guy, he thought, then froze. *Lucky guy?* Being a husband and father? Where had that come from all of a sudden?

Lucky because the redheaded beauty is his. That's all, Diego corrected himself.

"Hi, Robbie!" he heard a young voice say. Diego noticed a little boy, seven or eight, maybe, had come out of a room beside the bar, and smile up at the baby, clearly Robbie, and then the woman. Normally it wasn't the kind of place children hung out, but during this kind of celebration, The Tenacity Social Club was so family friendly that clearly a kid was not out of place.

"You okay, Jenna?" the bartender asked the woman as he pulled down the yellow hood to reveal a headful of wispy auburn curls. He kissed the little forehead, then rocked the baby a bit as he peered at the woman—with concern. Husbandly concern.

So her name was Jenna.

If Jenna responded, Diego couldn't hear. Suddenly she pivoted and rushed out.

Whoa. What was that about? The bartender didn't seem affected. He was lifting the baby up and down in a round of Upsy-Daisy, the little boy giggling and holding up his arms.

"Can you even lift me anymore?" the boy asked with a grin. "I *am* eight."

Hmm, were they a family? Of four? The mysterious, beautiful Jenna was a mother of two?

"I'll always be able to lift you, buddy," the bartender said, his gaze soft on the boy.

Diego watched the very sweet scene, wondering why such a caring man didn't seem to care about his wife, who'd run out with all that stress on her face.

Diego forced his attention back to the table, where talk had turned to the differences between Tenacity and Bronco, another Montana town where Stanley and Winona lived half the time. The Sanchezes had relatives there, but it was a good distance away.

Diego glanced toward the door, then back to the bartender, who was rocking the baby and humming a lullaby.

He couldn't stop thinking of Jenna's face—troubled. Not like: *My baby won't stop crying and it's driving me bonkers.* Or: *I'm so tired and need a twenty-minute nap.* Something was really bothering the woman. Diego wondered what.

Why *he* was so concerned about a stranger he'd seen for less than a minute was beyond him.

But he did care. Was she outside, leaning against the building covering her face with her hands, worrying about something? Was she pacing? Or had she left?

It was really cold out there. February in Montana. At night.

Diego was only half paying attention to conversation at the table—Stanley was saying it was time to go, that octogenarians and nonagenarians turned into pumpkins at ten thirty. The group started getting up, everyone hugging Marisa and Dawson, again saying what a beautiful wedding it had been.

Ah, time to go anyway. The perfect opportunity to check on Jenna.

And make sure she was okay. But if she wasn't out there, if she'd left, he'd worry about her all night.

Sometimes Diego really surprised himself. And this was one of those times.

Jenna Lattimore sat in her car in the parking lot of the Tenacity Social Club, staring at the puffs of air her breath was making in the cold. She was freezing but didn't turn on the ignition for heat. She couldn't move, couldn't think. She didn't want to think—that was the point.

Would this ever get easier?

Between the cold and the forecast—snow for the next couple of days, including a possible blizzard—Jenna couldn't stop the barrage of painful memories. Over a year ago, on a frigid December day, Jenna had lost her husband when a storm had turned into a blizzard and the whiteout had sent Rob Lattimore's pickup careening into a tree. He'd been going slow but it hadn't mattered. Just like that, he was gone.

A wife had lost her husband. A baby who hadn't even been born yet had lost her daddy.

Thirty minutes ago, Jenna had been standing with baby Robbie at the sliding doors to the patio in her house, pointing out the evergreens in the yard and explaining how they never lost their green needles. The weather forecast on the TV news she'd had on in the background had suddenly caught her attention. The meteorologist was talking about the impending blizzard. A chill had snaked up her spine, and she'd been frozen in place just as she was now.

Then sorrow had overtaken her. A heavy, suffocating sadness—with her precious daughter in her arms. Jenna had made a promise to herself, to Rob's memory and to their baby that she wouldn't ever lose it in front of little Robbie. Her best friend, Mike Cooper, had told her that if her anxiety got the best of her, she should bundle up Robbie and bring her to him so that Jenna could just sit with the pain until it passed. It never did quite pass, not exactly, but day by day, week by week, month by month, she'd been able to focus on remembrance instead of sorrow. Except for days like today. When the smell of snow in the air, the forecast of a blizzard, gripped her hard.

In an instant, two lives had changed. That added to the fear. That at any moment...

She'd gotten Robbie into her snowsuit and had driven over to the Tenacity Social Club, where Mike, a rancher, moonlighted as a bartender two to three times a week for extra money. One look at her face, knowledge of the coming storm, and he'd known she needed just fifteen minutes, a half hour, to get ahold of herself. He'd watch Robbie until her anxiety passed, until she was ready to come back in and get the baby girl and take her back home.

Jenna picked up her phone from the console and stared at the photo on her lock screen of her precious daughter. That helped ground her. She eyed the time. Just before 11:00 p.m. She'd sit here just a bit longer, then go back in. Mike was working and had his nephew with him; the last thing the man needed was a baby to rock while trying to pour a draft for a customer.

And Jenna needed to get home; she didn't want to be out on the roads with even *hours* to spare before the first flake fell in the morning.

She didn't drive in snow anymore.

Extra deep breath, like in Lamaze class, she told herself, hearing her mom's words. Her parents lived an hour and a half away in Bronco, where Jenna had grown up, but Jenna spoke to her mother every day. Sometimes, when she was scared about the future, about the here and now, she'd need to hear that soothing voice telling her she would be okay, that she could always move back home. To take a deep breath, feel what she felt and just wait it out. That the memories would always hurt but that she had people who loved her who were ready with a hug at any time.

She couldn't see moving back home with her folks— despite her money troubles. Rob hadn't had life insurance. They'd talked about it, and when they got the happy news that Jenna was pregnant, Rob had made an appointment with an insurance agent. But it was for the day *after* the accident. Jenna had the small, sweet Cape Cod–style house they'd painstakingly saved for. She couldn't imagine selling it and downsizing even further. The home was where she felt safe, and it was Robbie's legacy. She couldn't leave. Her job at a daycare center didn't pay all that well, but it covered her bills and she had free childcare, plus two great bosses. She just got by, and she was grateful she did.

Besides, Tenacity was home—and she felt comfortable here. For lots of reasons. A hardscrabble, blue-collar

town, full of hard-working people—ranchers, mostly—
many of whom barely scraped by. Most young people
couldn't wait to escape it. But there was something to
be said for a small town where everyone knew your
history and loved you in spite of it. Those who chose to
stay recognized the value of family and friendship and
staying true to your word. Jenna liked that. She vaguely
remembered that there had been some big to-do about
fifteen years ago—a family that had been run out of Tenacity over what she wasn't sure. Back then she'd been
too worried about making the grades to get a scholar-
ship to pay attention to local gossip.

Now, she leaned her head back and took that Lamaze-
like deep breath.

Okay. She would go back inside. She would get her
beloved little girl and go home.

A tap on the window startled her and Jenna almost
jumped.

She turned to see a very good-looking man bending down beside the window. The black suede Stetson
gave him away as a cowboy. He was dressed up in a
wool overcoat, a bolo tie against a white shirt just vis-
ible. Jenna was pretty sure he'd been sitting with the big
group in the club when she'd gone inside. They'd all been
dressed to the nines. Jenna couldn't remember the last
time she'd been out of jeans or yoga pants.

Some people came out of the club, and a woman
joined the cowboy, peering in through the window at her.

What was this about? Jenna sighed and opened the
door and got out. It was time to go in anyway. She closed
the car door and locked up, then eyed the cowboy.

"I'm Diego Sanchez and this is my sister Nina," he

said. "I just wondered if you need help since you were sitting in the car without the engine even running. And it's cold out here." He gave a shiver. "Is the car not starting?"

Jenna's eyes misted with tears. Darn it. The kindness undid her. She wasn't used to someone making a fuss over her like this. And to Jenna, this constituted a fuss. She had her bestie Mike here in Tenacity, of course, but she'd kept to herself the past year. She had a few friends, though, including her bosses at the daycare. But for the most part, she shied away from people, afraid to get close, to care.

"Should I go get your husband?" Diego asked, peering at her with such concern.

"I don't have a husband," she said, the words still sounding so wrong after more than a year. She stared down at the ground, a numbness saving her from crying in front of the cowboy.

He winced as though embarrassed that he'd made an assumption. "Your boyfriend, then—the bartender."

Ah. He'd clearly seen her talking to Mike and handing over Robbie to him, but two and two didn't equal four in this case. Jenna was still so overwhelmed that she didn't have it in her to explain who Mike was to her. "I'm fine," she said. "I was just heading back in to pick up my daughter."

Diego's head tilted. He seemed to be taking in what she'd said, thinking about something, and trying to reach a conclusion.

Nina wrapped her arm around the cowboy's. "We'd better get going. Everyone's waiting." She gave Jenna a sympathetic look as though she understood that Jenna needed to be alone. Women had a way of reading one another.

"If you're sure," Diego said to Jenna, still assessing her. He was looking at her so intently, with even deepened concern in his eyes. She'd wonder why he was so interested in the first place, but he'd seen her rush into a bar with her baby, hand her over to the bartender and then rush out to sit in her car in the cold without even turning on the ignition for heat. Of course he wanted to make sure she was all right.

Get it together, Jenna, she told herself. *You're making total strangers nervous for you.*

She nodded and tried to put something of a smile on her face, but she was sure she looked awkward.

Nina's own smile was warm when she said, "We'll just make sure you get inside okay."

There was that kindness again, which clearly ran in the family. Jenna looked at them both and nodded once more, then hurried toward the entrance as a few more people came out. Someone held the door open for her, and she turned back to see Diego holding up a hand in goodbye.

She was struck by it to the point that she couldn't move for a moment.

Without even meaning to, she held up her hand too. He smiled—a big, warm smile—but didn't move. She finally realized he was waiting for her to go inside first.

The cowboy's creed. The guy was a gentleman. And kind. Between that and the breathtaking smile, Jenna actually felt better, a little stronger. She was ready to get her daughter, to be present for her.

Thank you, Diego. She didn't know why, exactly, but

something about him, about his kindness, about the way he looked at her like he really saw her, made her feel okay again tonight.

Yes—thank you, Diego Sanchez. Even though she was sure she'd never see him again.

Chapter Two

"So do you and Ruby hang out at the Tenacity Social Club often?" Diego asked his brother Julian the next morning—with an ulterior motive. They were inside the barn on the ranch where Diego and his father worked, but Will Sanchez wasn't feeling well so Julian was pitching in since he wanted to go over the plans for his new ranch afterward. The barn was heated just enough that coats and gloves weren't necessary.

"The only place we hang out *often* is home," Julian said, pausing in his raking. "I like the social club, but it's more for teens than families during the day. And with the kids, we're not having many date nights. Last night was the first time we've been out in a while."

Diego nodded, trying to figure out another way to ask his brother if he knew anything about the bartender without outright asking. That would lead to questions. At this point, Diego only wanted answers when it came to Jenna. He wasn't even sure why he couldn't stop thinking about her. Wondering how she was doing. He didn't know a thing about her, other than that she had a baby. Maybe a son too. And that she sat in her car in dark, cold parking lots at night.

Her face rose to mind. He hadn't known she had such blue eyes until they'd been face-to-face outside. Blue eyes filled with something he couldn't figure out. Unease for sure, though.

Oh hell. He was just going to have come out and ask. "The bartender? Nice that the club is so family friendly—he even had his kids with him at work last night."

Julian looked puzzled. "Mike Cooper? He doesn't have kids. Oh—wait, he kind of does right now. He's guardian of his eight-year-old nephew while the boy's mom is working out of the country. Cody, I think his name is."

Nephew. Huh. So not Jenna's son.

"And he was holding a baby for a while there," Diego said. "Is the baby his? His girlfriend came in—long red hair?—and gave him the baby to hold for a while."

Again his brother looked puzzled. "Girlfriend? Mike? Definitely not since he's gay. I've seen the redhead around town with the baby and with Mike a few times. If anything, they're just friends."

Gay. Just friends.

A strange sense of relief came over him that Mike wasn't her boyfriend. Because Diego was interested and had been the minute he'd seen her.

He wanted to know more about her. He *had* to know more.

"What's with the twenty questions?" Julian asked, resuming raking. He stopped and stared at Diego for a long moment. "Wait a minute. Is this why you've been single for a while? Why you always say no to blind dates?"

Huh? Now Diego paused from raking the straw. He turned to his brother. "What are you talking about?"

"You're clearly interested in Mike."

"I'm interested in *Jenna*," Diego said. "The redhead."

"Ah." Julian continued raking, stepping farther into the stall. "Single mom with a baby. Didn't see that coming for you."

"Nothing's coming for me," Diego muttered. "I'm just… I don't know. She seemed upset last night. And then Nina and I talked to her outside the club for a bit. Jenna just seemed so stressed. I want to make sure she got home okay."

"Such a Good Samaritan," Julian teased.

"All right, dammit, I'm interested. Something about her…"

Something that had kept him up last night. He'd thought about Jenna on the way home. *At* home. When he'd gone to bed. When he'd woken up at just after 2:15 a.m., his throat parched.

Last night, when he and Nina had watched Jenna go inside the club, his sister had said, *Diego, you're such a good guy. The woman who finally wins your heart will be very lucky.*

He'd waited a beat to see if she'd laugh and sock him in the arm or something. But she didn't. He must have looked at her like she had three heads because she'd added, *Yes, I'm being serious. You should settle down, Diego. It's time. Yeah, you got hurt. But it was years ago now. Don't let that dictate the rest of your life.*

Luckily just then, their sister Marisa pulled Nina away for a hug; the newlyweds were heading out for their honeymoon. The conversation had thankfully ended.

Was it time? Would it ever be time? When some relatives were surprised that Uncle Stanley had fallen in love again after being widowed, the starry-eyed octogenarian had said: *You know what you know when you know it—and I know it.* Diego had understood. Except when it came to himself. At the moment he didn't feel much ready for anything other than a strong cup of coffee.

Julian was grinning now. "Well, little brother, let me help you out. I'm pretty sure her last name is Larrimore. No—*Lattimore*. With t's."

"Jenna Lattimore," he repeated. He'd look her up. Phone numbers and addresses were easy to find online. He'd call or even stop by. Just to check on her.

"Diego, when you need to know where to get diapers on sale or the best lullabies to sing a cranky baby to sleep, just ask." Julian started whistling a lullaby and resumed raking.

"Let's not get a million miles ahead of ourselves," Diego said, moving to the next stall. Good. He needed a little distance from what his brother was saying. Diapers? Lullabies? Come on.

Diego could hear a vehicle pulling up, so they both leaned their rakes against a post and put on their jackets, then went outside to see who it was. It was just flurrying now, but they were expecting a couple of inches by tonight and a storm tomorrow. He and Julian had started out even earlier than the usual pre-rooster crowing to make sure they'd get everything taken care of.

Luca, the youngest of the Sanchez brothers, got out of his pickup. He looked a lot like Diego and Julian. Same dark hair and eyes. Tall and muscular from years of ranch work.

"Hey," Luca said as he approached them outside the barn. "Thought I'd come see if you needed any help.

Dad mentioned you were filling in for him this morning." One of the benefits to living on the ranch where two Sanchezes worked was that if one was having an off day, another Sanchez was always willing to help out.

"Appreciate that," Diego said. "It's about time to get the cattle moved closer in." They started walking toward the barn to saddle up the horses.

"Oh and by the way, Luca," Julian said. "Diego's interested in a single woman with a baby." He shot Luca a grin.

Luca stopped in his tracks. "Good one," he said on a laugh.

Julian laughed. "I kid you not. He just said so himself."

Diego was the only one not smiling here. "I don't even know her! I'm just…curious about her. That's all."

At this point.

"Well, that's how it starts," Luca said. "And this from the guy who gave Julian a hard time about dating a single mother?" He clapped an arm around Diego.

"We both gave him a hard time," Diego reminded Luca. "And I wouldn't even call it that. We just pointed out that his life would change—hard and fast. That dating a single mother came with big responsibilities."

"Well, we'll tell *you* that now," Luca said. He turned to Julian as they each picked up a saddle. "Any words of wisdom for a guy who hasn't even had a *relationship* in years?"

"Hey, I've dated," Diego said.

"Yeah, maybe you've gone out with the same woman three times at most. And I can't recall any single or divorced mothers in the mix. So who's the lady? How old is her kid?"

Diego sighed and told Luca what happened last night to get him off his back. "So I'm just concerned about her. Maybe she needs help. Or a friend."

Both brothers smiled. "Well, you go check up on Jenna," Julian said. "Remember what I said about the diapers and lullabies. You'll be asking in a matter of days."

Luca cracked up.

Diego laid the saddle over the mare. He took in a deep breath, the familiar scent of the barn, of any barn, grounding him a bit in this unfamiliar territory. Of being unusually interested in someone. A single mother, at that.

You know what you know when you know it...

The only thing *he* knew for sure right now was that he would go check up on Jenna Lattimore.

He *had* to. He just wouldn't explore the why of that too deeply.

Diego had gone home for his twenty minute break—to think about calling Jenna. *Think* because every time he started to press in her number, which was as easy to find online as he'd figured, he stopped before the fourth number.

He sat on his bed and stared at the phone. *It's just a hello. A how are you? Just checking in since last night...* That wouldn't lead anywhere but her *I'm fine, thanks,* the rote answer to that question, and they'd probably not run into each other again.

Which was for the best. Diapers? Lullabies? *What?*

Those were words that weren't in Diego's immediate future. Maybe a few years down the road?

He could hear Julian and Luca now. *A few years down the road or now if you meet the right woman.*

Well, Jenna Lattimore couldn't be the right woman. She was a package deal. She had responsibilities. No way would she be interested in "just a cowboy."

Would he ever get that voice out of his head? Probably not.

Well, then he had no reason not to check in. To just hear that she was okay so he could somehow force himself to stop thinking about her.

Yes. Once he knew she was all right, that she'd just had a bad night, he'd go back to his regular old thoughts. His job. His family.

That he just might die alone, after all.

Dammit.

The problem with forcing himself not to think about Jenna was that she was so fully present in his mind. Her face, those beautiful eyes. Something about her had captured his attention. That was how attraction and chemistry worked—whether he liked it or not. Whether she was a single mother of a baby or not—not a carefree woman who might say yes to a date.

A date. That was something else he couldn't stop thinking about. Sitting across from Jenna at a restaurant. Having a drink, a good meal, talking, getting to know each other.

Oh yeah, he would like that.

But.

She'd find out during the *so what do you do* small talk on their date that he was "just a cowboy," and she'd rule him out.

He got up and sat back down. *What is with you? You*

saw this woman for like 5 minutes once in your life! Get a grip!

Except it *was* just five minutes—and she'd made *that* much of an impression.

Just call her. Check in. The call won't go anywhere. You'll go back to work. You'll wonder what Tio *Stanley is making for dinner, if it's his turn. You'll fix the broken hinge on the back door. You'll put Jenna out of your mind.*

He pressed in the numbers. All of them this time.

Voice mail. Ah, perfect. He hadn't even considered that, but he was calling her landline and she was probably off somewhere, town or at work.

He really liked the sound of her voice.

Leave a message after the beep and I'll return your call as soon as I can. Thanks!

"Hi, Jenna, it's Diego. Sanchez. We met last night outside the Tenacity Social Club. I was the nosy one wondering if you were okay? I guess I'm still wondering and just want to hear you got home fine and all is well with you. How about this, if all is well, no need to call me back. If you could use a friend, feel free to call me back." He left his number and then disconnected the call.

His heart was beating a little too fast. He stood up again and paced. He thought he'd gotten that voice mail right. No pressure to call him back.

Honestly, he didn't know which he preferred. A call back.

Or not.

Jenna had been home on her afternoon off, sitting in the kitchen with a mug of coffee and her laptop while

Robbie was napping when her phone had rung. The land-line. Caller ID showed it was an unknown number.

She'd let it go to voicemail, but the second she heard Diego's voice, heard him say his name, she'd almost jumped.

With nerves. And a little excitement. His very good looking face came to mind, his dark hair and dark eyes, the kindness in his expression. That he'd managed to ac-tually register at all during all that anxiety was some-thing. In a moment when she needed a strong hug, Diego Sanchez's gallantry had pretty much rescued her from herself.

There'd been a time or two or three even, when she'd been that anxious at a very inopportune time, like in the supermarket with a full cart, and a man had come over in the produce section to ask if she was okay, that she looked…stricken. She'd forced whatever pleasant expression she could and said she was fine and hurried off. No one had ever made an impression on her, except to appreciate a nice gesture toward her.

So why had Diego Sanchez managed to get in her head? Why was she picturing his face? Why had she listened to the voice mail a *second* time?

She was okay now. So there was no need to call him back.

She bit her lip. She *wanted* to call him back. The awareness of that jolted her and she stood up and paced some more.

What did this mean? She certainly couldn't be inter-ested in him, right?

Sure felt that way, though. Those happy little feelings

for a little crush. She'd had plenty of that in high school. Before she'd fallen hard for Rob Lattimore.

Her late husband's name in her thoughts had her sitting back down.

She bit her lip again.

There it was—she wasn't really okay. She'd lost her first and only love. Dating wasn't on her radar.

You're scared to even consider it, a voice said.

Yeah, for good reason. How could she ever start dating when any man who could possibly turn her head would also have the power to destroy her if something happened to him?

Exactly, she thought, shaking her head. She'd never make it back a second time.

And she had Robbie to think about.

And that had to be that.

She sipped her coffee, which had gone cold. If this was all settled in her mind now, if she would not call him back because she *was* okay and needed to stay that way for her daughter's sake, then why couldn't she stop thinking about Diego?

He was so kind and she should be kind back by calling him to say thanks. But that would possibly open up some kind of...*something*. She didn't know what. Friendship? Friendship was good.

But what if he asked her out?

A small burst of butterflies suddenly fluttered in her belly. Could she possibly *want* him to?

She did, she realized. *You don't have to say yes. You probably won't say yes.* But the idea of it had a warmth now spreading in her chest.

She knew what to do. She would *not* call him back.

If "Unknown Number" called again, then she'd answer. If he did ask her out, she'd...see how she felt in the moment.

She was sure she'd say no—politely, nicely. She wasn't ready to date. Certainly not a man who'd managed to actually turn her head.

Luckily, Robbie chose that moment to wake from her nap with a hearty cry. Jenna vowed not to think about Diego again—if he did he call, she'd...see what happened.

But he probably wouldn't. He only expected her to call if she wasn't okay, if she needed a friend. If she didn't call to acknowledge that he'd left that nice voicemail, he wouldn't reach out again.

And as she picked up her baby girl, cuddling her close with a soft pat on her back, Jenna realized with a shocking burst of clarity that she hoped he *would* call again.

Chapter Three

The next day, with Robbie down for her morning nap, Jenna sat at the round table by the window in the kitchen with her laptop, phone and a mug of coffee—just like yesterday except the phone hadn't rung with an unknown number.

She was actually relieved.

And slightly disappointed.

Not that she had the right to be.

Focus, Jenna, she ordered herself. She had the morning off and was going over her budget to see where she could cut back. She glanced at her banking portal at her paltry savings, then at her checking account balance, low after paying the first of the month's bills. She also needed to bring in more money. She'd asked the owners of the daycare about taking on a couple more hours a day, but they were fully staffed and so that wasn't an option.

Mortgage. Phone. Electric. Gas. The forty bucks a storm she paid the cowboy down the road for plowing snow from her driveway—and in winter, those added up. Homeowner's insurance. Health insurance. She'd already canceled her internet and cable service since she had Wi-fi on her cell phone. She didn't see what else she could scale back. The car was paid for and upkeep wasn't too bad. She got her dental cleanings at the local university's dental school for 40 percent off the typical cost. She clipped digital coupons for the grocery store and shopped wisely. Babies were expensive, but Jenna had done well with some secondhand items in great condition, and Robbie had what she needed. Jenna bought diapers and baby food in bulk when she did a monthly shopping at a big box store a few towns over.

She took a sip of her coffee and pulled her laptop closer. She opened a Word document she'd started a few weeks ago. *Possible Side Gigs I Can Do at Home* was the heading. The list wasn't long. Hand-knitted items. Pies. Custom pizzas. Playlists.

She sighed. There was hardly a market in Tenacity for hand-knitted baby booties or caps. Or for specialty pizzas with every imaginable topping when everyone was fine with the plain and pepperoni at Pete's Pizza. And the Silver Spur Café always had a few pie choices every day and wasn't looking for freelance bakers either—she'd asked. Forget about her worst idea of making playlists for joggers or car rides or podcast lists by interest when folks could easily do that themselves with a few clicks.

At least she *did* get by. She could pay her bills. There just wasn't money for extras. Like the lullaby-playing bouncer she wished she could buy for Robbie, let alone an extra pacifier to keep upstairs. $4.99 for a plain pink binky was a no-go when money was tight and she had a perfectly good one.

Jenna's gaze drifted out the window, the flurries not getting to her. Surprised, she sat up straight and stared out at the pretty white flakes drifting and settling on the evergreen out front. When was the last time she'd thought of snow as pretty?

Granted, it wasn't snowing hard by any stretch. But the day before yesterday, just the mention of the storm coming had sent Jenna into a downward spiral of memories and fear.

It's the cowboy.

Diego Sanchez.

His good will—his and his sister's kindness—had stayed with her. As had his follow-up call and voice mail.

And warm dark eyes. It was the darndest thing, but on the way home two nights ago from the Tenacity Social Club with Robbie safely buckled into her rear-facing car seat, and for hours afterward, any time Jenna would get nervous about the forecast, Diego's face would float into her mind and she'd feel a little better.

She pulled her long green cardigan more tightly around her. She wasn't sure why he'd made such an impression. Yes, he'd been nice. But it was more than that. If she was being honest with herself, she'd admit to... finding him attractive. Very much so. To the point that last night, as she'd lain in bed, she'd wondered what it would be like for those strong cowboy arms to hold her.

She sucked in a breath. Jenna hadn't thought about dating at all—not once. Rob Lattimore had been a great guy, a great husband. They'd been together since college, where she'd also met Mike Cooper. At first Rob had been jealous of her growing friendship with the tall, handsome guy until Jenna had shared that Mike's romantic interests were elsewhere—like on the cute guy in their history class.

Both Rob and Mike were from Tenacity but hadn't known each other despite how small the town was. Different circles. Rob had wanted to settle down in Tenacity because his widowed mom had been ill, so they had, but unfortunately, they'd lost her soon after they bought the house. Rob had felt the connection to his parents strongly in town, so they'd stayed, and since Mike lived there too, Jenna had even more reason not to fight for moving to Bronco, where she'd grown up. It was just far enough away at an hour and a half to make it difficult to see her parents, for them to see their grandbaby. But in the year that Rob had been gone, she couldn't imagine leaving. Not only was the house her baby's legacy, but she felt settled here.

She loved Tenacity. Here and there over the years, some stores had closed, but those that had managed to stay in business were beloved by the ranching community. While Tenacity was a town used to hard times, it was still a place where neighbors helped each other.

She felt safe here. She had Mike, and her job, and nice neighbors. And she'd recently made a new friend. Renee Trent owned a mobile dog grooming business and had clients on this road. They'd started chatting when Renee had been giving a huge poodle a bath in the yard a couple houses down. One day, Jenna would get a puppy to add to the family. That was all the extra love she'd be up for.

She was *not* ready to date.

She looked out the window at the flurries, coming down a bit harder now. She was a Big Sky girl, and there was no getting away from snow—and lots of it—in Montana. She'd have to make peace with it. Somehow. But as the wind began whipping the flurries around, she started getting that panicky feeling again.

Diego Sanchez's good-looking face, his strong shoulders in that wool overcoat, came to mind and she felt herself relaxing.

He was like her own secret talisman of sorts. She had a sudden urge to tell him how grateful she was for the way he and his sister had been so kind that night. For caring. For asking. For being there. For watching her go inside, safe and sound. The way her husband would have.

She bit her lip. She sure seemed interested in this man. In a *romantic* way.

Was that what these feeling were about? And was that okay?

She grabbed her phone and called Mike. He'd be working on his family ranch right now, his nephew in school. Especially with his twin sister away, Mike had his hands full, and he'd confided in Jenna that times were tough for Cooper Ranch. He often told her he appreciated being able to take a break when he got a call. If he was busy with cattle or a horse or riding fences, he'd let her know he'd have to call her back.

"Hey, Jenna," Mike said. "I was just about to check in with you. You doing okay?"

When she'd gotten home from the club the other night she'd texted him to let him know she'd arrived and he'd asked that same question. You doing okay? She'd texted back that she was. And for the first time in a long while, that had actually been the truth.

"Strangest thing, Mike," she said. Should she even say it out loud? Wasn't that what best friends were for? To really talk to? "I, uh, met someone that night. In the half hour between dropping off Robbie and picking her up."

"You *did* seem a lot calmer when you came back in to get her," Mike said. "The color was back in your face. And not from the cold, either. But how did you possibly meet someone by sitting in your car in the parking lot?"

She told him the story. The knock on the window. The Sanchezes, all dressed up. The care and kindness. Diego holding up a hand in a wave as he'd waited for her to go in the club.

She didn't mention her attraction. She wasn't quite ready to say that aloud. Or to believe it herself, really.

Mike was quiet for a moment. "I don't know Diego personally, but I've heard a few women at the bar talking about him over the years," he finally said. Kind of cautiously. As though he was holding back.

"And saying what?" she asked. Mike always kept mum about what he overheard at the bar—or was told directly by a forlorn customer—but he'd mentioned more than once that the things he heard on a weekly basis sometimes made him glad he was single.

She swallowed around the sudden lump in her throat. Her very first foray into feeling the slightest bit of attraction for another man—and he was trouble?

"Okay, Jenna, you know I don't gossip. I don't talk about what I overhear. But you're my best friend. And so I'm just going to tell you that I've heard a few different women say that Diego Sanchez doesn't commit, that he never goes out with the same woman more than a couple times."

Her heart plummeted. "He's a player?"

"I don't know about that, necessarily, but apparently, he's not looking for a relationship."

"Oh," she said.

Well, I'm not either, right?

"I do know he comes from a great family. I'm not surprised he and his sister came to your rescue. But maybe he's not someone to get interested in."

That was coming a little late.

"Well, I'm hardly ready for a relationship," she said. "Maybe a first step back into that world with someone gorgeous and sexy and kind is what I need. Then when our two or three dates are up, we go our separate ways."

"Listen, honey. It's not that I don't think you're ready to start thinking about dating. But your heart is delicate, Jenna. You need someone who'll be careful with it."

That was probably true too.

Robbie let out a cry. Jenna waited a beat since the baby girl had gotten adept at soothing herself back to sleep if something woke her up. *"Waah! Waah!"*

"I hear my favorite baby," Mike said.

"I'd better go get her. I'll talk to you later."

"Jenna, sorry if I was the bearer of bad news. I just love you, you know?"

Her heart swelled. "I know, Mike. And I love you too."

They disconnected and she headed down the hall to the nursery. Robbie's room was small but sweet, painted a pale yellow since she and Rob had wanted to be surprised with the sex. When it came time to paint the room, Jenna had opted for a neutral color scheme. Rob had never gotten to know his baby was a girl.

One more fussy cry came from the crib. Jenna reached in and scooped up her daughter, cuddling her close.

"Well, maybe it's for the best that Diego Sanchez isn't up for a relationship," she said to Robbie as she laid her down on the changing table. "Because I'm not either."

With Robbie's diaper changed, she brought the baby into the living room. Her phone rang—the landline.

Unknown caller.

Jenna's heart was practically bursting out of her chest.

She set Robbie in her playpen and sucked in a breath—and then picked up the receiver.

Oh God. "Hello?" she said, wondering if she sounded nervous. For all she knew it wasn't even him. Maybe it was a spam call.

"Hi, Jenna, it's Diego Sanchez. We met two nights ago?"

She almost gasped. Not spam. *Him.*

I was just talking about you... Ears burning, maybe?

"Hi," she said. "I'm glad you called back."

"Oh?"

"I wanted to thank you for the other night. For being concerned. You and your sister. I really appreciated it. I was in a bad way and your kindness snapped me out of it. I was okay yesterday and that's why I didn't call back. But thank you."

"You're welcome. And I'm extra glad I went to check on you in your car." Diego was silent for a moment, as though he was waiting for her to elaborate, fill in some missing information. But she was kind of speechless at the moment. A little shocked that he'd called just when she'd been talking about him. Thinking about him. For two days now.

"I'm sorry for being so curt," she said. "You would have no way of knowing this but—"

She stopped talking, her heart suddenly pounding. She wasn't sure what was going on. Nerves, probably. The attraction. And what Mike had said.

"Knowing what?" he asked.

She bit her lip. "That… I'm a widow. I lost my husband in a car accident a little over a year ago. In a snowstorm. I heard the forecast, and I got so anxious." She explained how they had an understanding that when she felt that way, she'd bring Robbie to him so she could get through the difficult moment without her daughter in her arms.

"Oh, Jenna. I'm so sorry. Everything about that night makes sense now."

She took in a deep breath.

"My family's in Bronco. And Rob—my late husband—his family is gone. So it's just me and Robbie. And Mike, thank heavens. I'm just trying to figure things out, you know? How to get by."

"I understand," Diego said. "Getting by is tough when your heart is broken and the world feels tilted. When you wake up and put on a brave face but feel scared inside."

She almost gasped again. "Yes, that's exactly how I feel." How could he know that? She hadn't even been able to articulate to her parents how she'd been feeling all these months. Maybe because she didn't want to worry them. And here she was telling a near stranger her most private thoughts. Making herself vulnerable. And he got it.

"You've lost someone close to you?" she asked, knowing he had. In some way or another.

"Not like you," he said. "Let's just say I've had my heart handed back to me. Cruelly."

She winced. She barely knew Diego Sanchez, and she'd felt that *cruelly* in all her nerve endings. He'd been hurt bad. "I'm sorry about that," she said.

"It was a while ago. You'd think I'd be over it but—" He stopped. "Now wait a minute. I've known you for barely two days. I've talked to you for like ten minutes total. And I'm spilling my guts? What secret powers do you have, Jenna Lattimore?"

He knew her last name. Which meant he'd done a little work to track her down, find her number.

He'd reached out *again* too.

She felt her smile in her toes.

"I could say the same for you, Diego."

They talked some more, about the Tenacity Social Club and how it had once been a speakeasy, like a hundred years ago. That he'd been there only twice, the first time because his uncle Stanley had insisted the whole family go for karaoke night, and then just yesterday for a nightcap celebration after his sister's wedding.

"I have to say, the nachos were pretty good," Diego said.

"Mike's nephew Cody loves those nachos," she said. And suddenly there were talking about their favorite places in Tenacity, both agreeing there weren't many options but that the Silver Spur Café had good burgers and pie, but they were only open for breakfast and lunch.

"I have a question for you," he said.

Butterflies let loose in her stomach. She liked Diego Sanchez a little too much if she was excited by a pending random question. "I'm all ears."

"I'd like to take you out," he said. "To dinner. Or whatever you might like. I guess that's more a statement than a question. But I'm asking you on a date, Jenna. I'd suggest a casual walk in the park but it's freezing and—"

And a snowstorm is coming. She could hear him about to say it and then remembering what she'd said earlier about how snowstorms affected her.

A snowstorm *was* coming. And maybe this was all just moving too fast.

Who was she kidding about being ready for any of this? Even flirting was apparently too much for her.

"I, uh, it's probably, um…" *Oh God, Jenna. Just speak.* "A formal date might be too much. But a walk in the park is out too. So it's probably a sign that…" She trailed off, not quite ready to say no entirely either.

She *did* like this man. Yesterday, after his voice mail, she'd tried so hard to put him out of her head. But she kept seeing his handsome face, hearing his voice.

"I know just the thing, then," he said, clearly running with the opening she'd given him. "I'll bring over dinner. We can sit on the sofa with our plates on our laps. Watch a sitcom or a movie. And Robbie is invited too, of course. I can even bring a jar of her favorite baby food."

Her toes tingled again. She liked that idea. A lot.

"Robbie does like pureed sweet potatoes," she said.

He laughed. "Don't we all."

She heard herself laugh too. She didn't do much of that these days.

"It's a date then," she said, then swallowed, the word sounding so formal. "Or something," she added fast.

"Or something," he repeated, his voice warm. "How about Thursday night?"

The day after tomorrow. "Sure."

If they did get a bad snowstorm, he'd cancel. Then she could breathe easy. Either way, it was win-win.

A baby step into almost dating—*or something.*

Chapter Four

That night, the Sanchezes were together again—minus Marisa who was away on her honeymoon—this time for dinner at the family home. Sometimes Diego wondered how the seven of them—his mom, dad and the five kids—had fit into this house. There were three bedrooms—the girls had shared one room, the boys another, and his parents had the primary. There were two bathrooms, at least, not that his sisters in particular had found two enough. But step outside on the ranch and they had all the space they needed. The place might not be theirs—Will and Nicole had long rented the "large hands cabin"—but they'd turned it into a cozy home, and all that land and sky out the front door, the mountains in the background, felt like it stretched on forever.

"So what's this I hear about Diego dating a single mom of a baby?" Nina asked, mirth in her eyes. She twirled a forkful of pasta.

Uh-oh. Diego was not interested in being the topic of conversation again. His appetite for his mother's always scrumptious meatballs and linguini was waning.

And how could this possibly have gotten out? He hadn't told anyone about the date.

Luca had the decency to look guilty. "Hey, I only said he was *interested* in Jenna Lattimore." He turned to Diego. "I ran into Nina and Mom in town earlier and it just popped out."

"Oh, I'm sure," Diego said, shaking his head with a smile. "But if you must know, we *do* have a date. Thursday night."

Nina gasped. "Thursday night? Really? Wow."

Diego frowned, his fork paused midway to his mouth. "What's the big deal about Thursday?" He'd always thought weekend nights were the biggies for dates.

"Even *I* know what the big deal is," Luca said, taking a piece of garlic bread from the basket in the center of the table. "And I don't have a date."

"Well, someone fill me in," Diego said, staring around the table at his relatives. They were all looking at him like he was from another planet.

"Thursday," Ruby said, "is Valentine's Day."

Now it was Diego's turn to gasp. "Oh. *Ohhh*."

"Yeah," Nina continued. "A first date on Valentine's Day? Unusual unless both parties are *really* into each other." She wiggled her eyebrows at him.

"You must really like this woman," Nicole Sanchez said, something like relief in his mother's dark eyes. She'd made it clear she wanted to see all her children happy and settled. Two down, three to go.

He had to change the subject—fast. That this was the topic of conversation was bad enough, but the date was scheduled for Valentine's Day? Why hadn't he checked a calendar first?

Then again, Jenna hadn't seemed to know either—or care. She'd been widowed just over a year ago. Valentine's Day was probably the last thing on her mind. Unless it *was*—and added to her sadness the other night.

His heart lurched for her.

Diego had loved and lost hard—but not to that degree. Not a spouse. He glanced at his uncle Stanley, who was clearly enjoying the conversation. Diego would never forget how devastated his uncle had been when he'd lost his wife of sixty years. Sixty years! Not to mention the gut-wrenching pain he'd gone through when he thought he'd lost Winona last year after she'd vanished without a trace on their wedding day. But now here Stanley was, his arm around his bride, happiness on Stanley's lined face that lifted Diego's spirits on a daily basis. There were second chances at love. If you were willing and open.

He wondered if Jenna was.

Was *he*? All he knew was that he was very interested in Jenna.

"So maybe Diego will be the next Sanchez to walk down the aisle, after all," Uncle Stanley said. He raised his glass, and everyone else did too, clinking away while Diego felt a punch to his stomach.

Marriage? Well, that was taking things a giant step too far. What did he have to offer a single mother with the huge responsibility of a baby? He didn't have his own home. He didn't have his own ranch.

You'll always be just a cowboy on some middling ranch...

I have big dreams...

Diego slunk down in his chair, his appetite gone.

Maybe this was a mistake. But there was no way he'd cancel the date when she'd already accepted.

Over their cheeseburgers or turkey clubs on her sofa tomorrow night, she'd very likely bring up at some opportune point that she wasn't interested in anything beyond friendship, that she needed a different kind of man. A family man. A man who could make her feel safe, secure. A man with something to offer a widow and her baby.

Yes. He was getting ahead of himself again. But for good reason. She'd shut this down at the end of the date and they'd be friends.

Except there was no way he could see being platonic with beautiful, sexy Jenna Lattimore.

From the moment Jenna had ended the call with Diego Sanchez yesterday to now she'd been going back and forth about the date. *I should cancel. I should not cancel. It's too much. It's just enough.*

As she stood at a big round table in the Little Cowpokes Daycare Center, collecting crayons the kiddos had left scattered during arts and crafts, she made a final decision. She wasn't canceling.

She'd learned over the years that when she was on the fence about something, she should just accept that something was holding her back for a reason.

So she hadn't picked up her phone to call him and say she just wasn't ready.

She wasn't—but she wanted to take that baby step. Not in general. *That* she did understand.

With Diego. Specifically.

There was just something special about him. Something she couldn't ignore if she wanted to.

She'd see how it went, minute by minute. How it felt

to have a man in her house. On her sofa. Sharing a meal while watching a comedy. If it was too much, she'd know and be honest with herself and with Diego.

"The flurries are coming down harder," one of her bosses, Angela Corey, said, her gaze out the window. Seventy-two-year-old Angela, who Jenna adored, co-owned the daycare with Elaina Bernard, who was leading an end-of-day sing-along in the back room. Jenna glanced out the window, which she'd been avoiding since a light snow had started a half hour ago. Barely an inch of snow covered the grounds, the roads reasonably clear but dusted. Tomorrow's storm had been scaled back from potential storm to a few inches of snow. Which would hardly ever just be basic to her. She was glad she'd have company tomorrow night, when the roads should be kept clear. "Head home, honey," Angela said. "Elaina and I have it covered."

Relief swept through Jenna. "You sure?"

"Positive. And if it's bad tomorrow, don't even think about coming in. You hear?"

Thank God for Angela and Elaina, both so warm and compassionate. They knew about Jenna's loss and whenever it so much as flurried, they were by her side, checking in, offering a soothing cup of tea, making sure she was all right—as they'd been doing all day. She'd been wrong to think that Rob had been the last to make a fuss over her, to care if she got home safely. Yes, he'd been the last to make that fuss from a place of romantic love, but she knew how lucky she was to have this job with such wonderful bosses who'd become friends. She also knew she had to work on not letting the snow get to her.

After saying her goodbyes to the children now getting

ready for pickup, Jenna bundled up Robbie and headed out. She looked up at the sky, the white flakes falling all around her. Once she'd found snow so beautiful. She hoped she would again.

All in time, she told herself.

Yesterday she'd thought the flurries were pretty. A good start. The blossoming of possibilities.

A few minutes later, driving five miles an hour down Central Avenue, Jenna was feeling less friendly toward the snow. The wind picked up and a few times she'd had to use her windshield wipers just to see past the blowing flakes. Her chest tightened.

Honk!

Jenna almost jumped and glanced in the rearview mirror. A small dark car was too close. Jerk! She put on her blinker and pulled over to the shoulder so they could pass. As the car peeled off as though the roads were perfectly dry, Jenna sucked in a few sharp breaths, looking in the back seat to check on Robbie. But since the car seat was rear-facing she couldn't see her daughter's face. She needed to. Just see her sweet face. Jenna quickly got out and went to the back door, opening it up and peering in. Her baby girl was looking at her, curious and alert, happy. Jenna took a calming breath. *Everything is okay. You're okay. Just drive slowly.*

She was about to get back in her car when a pickup truck pulled up behind her, the door opening and someone hurrying out toward her.

A tall, muscular man in a dark brown cowboy hat, the snow collecting on the brim and the broad shoulders of his navy blue down jacket.

Diego Sanchez.

"Jenna! I recognized your car. Are you okay? Did your car slide off the road?" He stopped close by, peering at her, then studying her car, checking the tires. Checking her face, her eyes. He suddenly looked in the rear window at the car seat, and the concern on his face truly moved her.

"I'm fine," she quickly assured him. "As is Robbie. The car is fine too. I was going so slow a car honked at me, and I pulled over to let him pass and then…" She bit her lip. Tears sprung to her eyes. She hated how she sounded. Weak. Like a woman who couldn't handle herself, her life. She was someone's mother, this baby's only parent. She had to be better than this, stronger. "I'm fine, really."

But she wasn't. She was trying, but she wasn't fine.

There were flurries on her eyelashes. On her nose. She wanted to cry.

He reached for her hand and gave it a quick squeeze. "I'll follow you home. Just to make sure you get there safe."

Relief came over her, unknotting her shoulders. "I hate to trouble you, Diego. But I won't say no to that. Thank you."

He smiled. That warm, dazzling smile that for just a moment made her completely forget everything, that she was standing outside on the side of the road, the snow coming down steadily now, despite the forecast calling for it to start later. "Of course. And if anyone honks me, I'll make sure their license plate appears in that online gossip column, the *Tenacity Tattler,* in a not-so-blind item about jerk drivers."

She actually managed to laugh. *Oh, Diego.* She got

back in her car, feeling warm and safe—and not alone. She turned on her blinker and pulled out, driving super slow. Diego stayed a good two cars distance behind her. There were a few cars behind him too, and maybe it was the big pickup or the tall, strong cowboy who owned it, but no one dared honk at *him*.

It took an extra ten minutes to get home. She pulled in her driveway, again flooded with relief. She was home safe. Her own hero cowboy pulling in beside her.

But then she noticed the tree down and half blocking the road a few houses up the road Were those power lines dangling by it?

That panicky feeling returned, her chest tightening again, her shoulders bunching up.

She stepped out into the windy night, the snow whipping around. She carefully got Robbie and shielded her face.

Diego stepped from his pickup and hurried over, holding up his phone. The screen was dark. "I'd just sent a text to my mom that I followed a friend home out of caution so not to expect me for dinner, but it looks like the wind and the wet snow took out cell service right after. And judging from the dark houses," he added, looking across the street, "the power might be out too."

Chills ran up her spine and she sucked in a breath. "The good news is that I have a fireplace and a good amount of logs piled up. And a bunch of flashlights. The house is small enough that it'll warm up fast."

A low heavy branch of the big tree in the yard was swaying near the driveway. Jenna almost screamed.

"You two head inside," he said, glancing up at the

tree, then back at her. "I'll take care of that branch. I have tools in my truck."

Jenna hurried the baby to the porch, got her key in the lock and opened the door. The power had clearly gone out recently because it was still warm inside. That was a relief, even if it was dark.

She got Robbie out of her snowsuit and cuddled her then went to the kitchen for a flashlight. She settled Robbie in her baby seat near the sofa while she lit a few candles on the mantel, the coffee table and in the kitchen. That was better. She scooped Robbie back up and moved to the window, watching as Diego carried some items from his truck over to the tree in the front yard near the driveway.

The snow, mixed with sleet, was coming down harder, the wind merciless. Diego had to be soaked, even in that down jacket and his cowboy hat. He had on a hard hat with a light in the center, a stepladder set up, and then used a big pair of clippers to take off the branch. A minute later, he was back, dripping wet on her doorstep, still in the hard hat.

"Hurry in," she said, shutting the door behind him.

He set the hard hat with the light shining on the narrow bench by the door, illuminating the small entryway and living room beyond.

She ran to the bathroom for a thick towel. As she watched him hang his hat on the coat rack and then use the towel on his face and wet hair, she suddenly envisioned him in the shower. Naked.

Whoa. What the heck?

She was going to have to accept that she was *very* attracted to Diego if she was picturing him naked in the middle of a snowstorm and power outage. Normally, she'd be fretting and pacing, despite her collection of flashlights and nonperishables and the fireplace.

He hung up the towel, then got out of his coat. He wore a dark green Henley shirt that showed off his broad shoulders, worn jeans and work boots.

At least she was more focused on him than on the storm. Not that it was doing all that much for her heart rate and stress. Could she actually be interested in another man? All signs said yes. Maybe this was how it happened. Every day pretty much like the last until you met someone who changed everything by just appearing.

She cleared her throat, trying to clear her head as well. "This is Robbie," she said, giving the baby a little bounce in her arms. "She'll be seven months tomorrow."

Valentine's Day.

She swallowed.

Tomorrow was Valentine's Day!

Their date. A very casual one, but still. She hadn't been thinking. Clearly, neither had he.

It's just take-out on the sofa, she reminded herself.

The warm smile Diego bestowed on the baby went straight to her heart. "Hi, sweetie. What a beauty you are." He covered his face with his hands, then opened them in a round of peekaboo. "Peekaboo, I see you!"

Robbie stared at him with those curious blue eyes and batted her hand toward him. "Ba! La!"

Jenna laughed. "She's been babbling for a couple of months now. I can't wait till she says *mama*!"

He smiled and very gently "shook" Robbie's hand with two fingers. "I'm Diego. It's very nice to meet you."

"You're good with babies!" The man might not be up

for a relationship, according to Mike, but he was nice to kids. Duly noted.

"From visiting my soon-to-be baby nephew and little niece," he said. "My brother Julian's girlfriend is a single mom with a four-year-old daughter, Emery, and she's in the process of adopting an adorable baby named Jay. I've been helping Julian plan out a ranch on land he just bought, so I've gotten to spend a lot of time with them the past couple of weeks."

Jenna smiled. "I've definitely seen them around town and at the playground. Last summer and fall I took Robbie to the playground a lot even though she couldn't exactly leave her stroller. It's just nice to sit on the bench in the sun among the other families."

Except that it was hard to watch daddies lift up their children into the baby swings. Wait by the bottom of the slide for their toddler to come happily shrieking down.

The wind was gusting so loudly that they both looked toward the living room window, where the trees were swaying, the snow whipping fast and furious.

"Diego, I know the plan was for you to come over tomorrow night, but since you're here and it's so bad out, how about I make us dinner? I'd feel better knowing you weren't out there driving."

"Only if you let me help," he said.

"Deal." Goose bumps broke out on her arm. "Though without power, we'll have to stick with sandwiches. You can choose between slathering the bread with the peanut butter or the jelly."

He laughed. "I'll do the jelly."

She laughed too. "Do you mind holding Robbie while I get the fire going?"

Did he wince slightly or was she imagining that? The discomfort on his face was gone before she could study him closely. She'd gotten the sense he was used to holding baby Jay and was comfortable or she wouldn't have put him on the spot.

"Sure," he said, reaching his arms out.

Robbie went right to him, no fuss and she was often fussy about people she wasn't familiar with. Her blue eyes latched on to him so fiercely that he smiled.

"She likes me," he said, his dark eyes sparkling with surprise.

Who wouldn't? she almost blurted out but thankfully didn't.

In a couple of hours, it would be Robbie's bedtime and then it would be just the two of them. Having that almost-a-date a night early.

With a blazing fire, which she was now lighting in the fireplace. On the sofa with their peanut butter and jelly sandwiches, cozy and warm and safe from the storm.

And now, her nerves had less to do with the snow than the fact that she was on what felt very much like a date.

Chapter Five

The moment Diego had little Robbie in his arms he felt a surge of protectiveness he hadn't expected. Similar to what watching Jenna in the Tenacity Social Club had engendered in him. Seeing her sitting in her cold dark car in the parking lot. And standing outside next to her car on Central Avenue earlier. With the snow coming down.

But this was something else. Something more. Probably because Robbie was a baby. Most likely because he was *holding* the baby.

Yes, that had to be what this was about. When he'd held Ruby's baby Jay, when he'd picked up little Emery to show her the star on the family's Christmas tree, he'd been hit with: *If you ever need anything, Uncle Diego is there. Anything at all.* And they weren't even officially his niece and nephew yet.

He'd better not so much as hug Jenna for ten seconds because he'd be a goner.

"You mommy is good at lighting a fire," he said to Robbie as he watched the flames begin to roar to life. Then he wished he hadn't said that aloud. Jenna had lit something inside him—that was for sure.

He quickly started telling Robbie how his dad had

taught him and his siblings to light a fire while they'd been camping far out on the ranch as children. Maybe Jenna wouldn't have taken what he'd said as an innuendo, anyway. He shouldn't be flirting with Jenna like that, not that he'd meant to. He had a great deal of respect for where she was right now, what she was going through.

Jenna turned and smiled, then gave the logs one last jab with the iron poker. She stood and walked over. "I'll take her."

He couldn't tell from her expression if he'd offended her. Maybe that meant he had.

He was about to make some awkward attempt at apology when she reached out her arms, but the second he'd handed the baby over he felt Robbie's absence and missed the sturdy little weight.

"Ready for a sandwich?" she asked him, giving the baby a kiss on top of her head. She smiled at him then, warmly. Relief unbunched his shoulders. She was letting the comment go. And so would he.

"Starving, actually." He grabbed the hard hat with the built-in light. "So we can see what we're doing." *So I can see your beautiful face*, he added silently.

She led the way to the kitchen, where she set Robbie down in her baby bouncer in the corner. Jenna gave Robbie a teething toy, which she began nibbling.

He set the hard hat on the counter and watched her take out the loaf of bread, the jars of peanut butter and strawberry jelly. He moved beside her as she set out two plates and two knives.

She placed two pieces of bread on each of their plates. "I like a lot of jelly, by the way."

"Me too," he said, and generously slathered both slices of the bread with jelly as she did the same with the peanut butter.

She laid both her pieces on top of his. "Voilà."

He cut both sandwiches in half, and took a bite. "Delicious. Never fails. Like french fries."

Jenna nodded and also took a bite. "Agree. I'm always surprised when pizza is bad. Like bad frozen pizza, I mean. It should always be good."

"Exactly," he said.

She looked too beautiful in the dimly lit kitchen. He could stand here and take in every bit of her, from her long silky red hair to her blue eyes and lush lips. She had delicate features and a sexy, lush figure. He had such an urge to take her in his arms and kiss her.

"I have to keep the fridge closed just in case the power doesn't come back on soon," she said, shaking him out of his trance. "But I have a bottle of sparkling water in the pantry if you'd like some."

"That sounds great."

She got out the bottle and poured two glasses.

He held up his glass. "To silver linings."

Surprise lit her eyes. "What's the silver lining here?"

"Bad storm. No power. But I'm exactly where I want to be. Doing exactly what I want to be doing."

She smiled. "Eating peanut butter and jelly in the dark—while standing at my kitchen counter?" Her smile faded a bit, and she was barely looking at him.

She's afraid, he realized. *This is all new to her. Be gentle*.

"With you," he said. There it was. Yeah, he'd asked

her out, so she knew he was interested. But he'd made something very clear just now. To both of them.

Prepare yourself to hear that she's not ready, he told himself. *It's likely what she's about to say.*

She bit her lip and looked at him, holding up her glass to his.

He realized he was holding his breath.

"To silver linings," she said, and clinked her glass with his.

He was so happily surprised that he wanted to step closer and reach a hand to her face, that urge to touch her, to *kiss* her, so strong.

But she took a sip of her water just then, her lips busy. He sipped too. Then she carried her plate to the table and sat down, so he did the same. There were four chairs at the round table and he opted for one right next to her.

It's better that you don't make a move, he told himself. *Jenna Lattimore isn't the typical woman you'd date. She's a widowed mother. Tread very carefully here.*

"Robbie sure likes that teether," he said, eyeing the baby gnawing away at the translucent green rubbery star.

"Loves it. Her first tooth is coming in. I'm so excited for her first word. I do hope it's *mama*, but I've heard some babies say all sorts of other words first, like *duck*."

"What was your first word?" he asked, then took a bite of his sandwich.

She smiled. "I actually know because my mother told me a few weeks ago when we were talking about exactly this. It was *dada*. She said her feelings were a little hurt." She laughed, but then stopped suddenly, her smile fading hard. "I guess that won't be Robbie's first word, though." She put her sandwich down and looked toward her lap, a sadness overtaking her face.

"Hey," he said gently. "Robbie's father is always going to be with her here." He tapped his chest in the region of his heart. "So it very well might be her first word. Don't get offended like your mom, though," he teased.

She brightened a bit and looked at him. "I hope you're right."

"I'm sure you tell Robbie about her daddy all the time," he said. "While you're feeding her, you probably mention her father loved applesauce or scrambled eggs. And while you're bundling her up in her cute little yellow snowsuit, you probably tell her that he loved the color yellow."

"He did," she said with a hint of smile. "It's why I chose that snowsuit."

He reached his hand over and gave hers a squeeze. "He's with her all the time because of you."

She burst into tears, which he hadn't been expecting. He got up and knelt down in front her.

"I'm sorry, Jenna. I shouldn't be saying anything." *Idiot*, he chastised himself. He had no business talking to a widowed mother about her late husband or her baby. Like he knew anything about what she was going through or feeling. Especially during a snowstorm.

She shook her head, wiping her eyes. She leaned toward him and wrapped her arms around him, resting her head on his shoulder.

He almost gasped at the intimacy of the gesture, the moment. Once again, he was holding his breath, unable to move a muscle.

"They're not sad tears," she said. "You said exactly

the right thing. I'm just very touched and a little emotional."

He felt himself loosening just then and hugged her back, vaguely aware of the scent of her shampoo. He could stay like this for hours.

But unfortunately, she lifted her head and sat back in her chair. He stood and went back to his.

She cleared her throat, and he knew she too needed a moment. "Thank you, Diego."

"Of course," he said. "And thank you for dinner."

She glanced at him before taking a sip of her water. "You're so…good at this. I'm surprised you're not married with three kids."

"Good at what?" he asked, tilting his head—and having no idea what she was going to say.

"People. Knowing when someone needs a kind word, a tender look, a squeeze of the hand. A hug."

"My siblings would be looking at you like you were from another planet," he said with a smile. "My brothers especially."

"Well, I speak from personal experience."

A warmth spread inside him. "I appreciate that."

She took a bite of her sandwich. "I really am surprised you're single, Diego Sanchez. You're a serious catch."

He winced and hoped it wasn't too evident. "I don't know about that. I thought I was headed in that direction once. But things didn't work out."

"You proposed?"

"Didn't get that far," he said. "We dated for six months, but I wasn't what she was looking for, so…"

She was staring at him intently. "What was she looking for?"

He wasn't expecting that question. Nor did he want to answer it. She'd know he was the same guy he was back then. Living at his family home, doing the same job. Seven years later, nothing had changed. His ex had been right.

At twenty-six, he'd had the excuse of still being young. At thirty-three, he was proving his ex right. Her friends must see him around town and think, *Wow, at first we thought she was being snobby, but turns out she was right. Dodged a bullet there...*

Diego Sanchez had nothing much to offer a woman—especially a single mother of a baby—except maybe that compassion Jenna had been talking about moments ago. That and fifty cents...

Luckily, Robbie started fussing and he'd never been so happy to hear a sharp cry come out of a baby. Saved by the shriek. Robbie rubbed her eyes as her mom picked her up.

"Someone's ready for bed," Jenna said, patting her daughter's back and murmuring to her. "It's a little early but tired is tired. I guess I'll move her bassinet into the living room where it'll be warm all night."

"I'll go get it," he said, shooting up.

"Upstairs, second door on the left. And thanks."

He headed up. The nursery was a soft yellow with stenciled white stars and moons on the walls. On the dresser was a photo of Jenna with a good-looking man with light brown hair and blue eyes. In a suit. Not a cowboy. Or blue collar. He could tell the photo had captured them as they usually were, because Jenna wore jeans and a T-shirt, so they weren't at an event that required dressing up.

He let himself look at the photo for a while. A widow with a baby who'd been married to a successful man needed a different kind of guy than Diego. He'd known that before he saw the photo, but it was all the more reason to not date Jenna Lattimore. Not fall for her. Because if he did—and he could see that happening—she'd get realistic in a couple of months and tell him she had a child to think about, sorry.

He waited for the usual bitterness to settle in his gut but all he felt was…disappointment. Not in Jenna. In *himself.*

He sucked in a breath and then picked up the bassinet and its stand and carried them downstairs.

"You're my hero, Diego Sanchez," she said. "You've come to my aid quite a few times for someone I just met two days ago."

I wish I could be your hero, he thought, then froze for a second. He knew he liked Jenna. That he was very attracted to her. That he felt protective toward her and Robbie. But would he be ready to date a woman with a child anyway?

If he were thirty-three and not a cowboy on someone *else's* ranch, sure. He'd have something to give, a home, roots, a legacy.

Robbie brought up a little fist and rubbed her eyes again. He shook away his thoughts. He might not be their hero, but he could help while he was here.

"Where would you like this?" he asked.

"How about that corner," she said, pointing. "She'll stay warm but won't be too close to the flames. And I can keep an eye on her. I'm always happiest when I can see her little face, you know?"

"I'll bet," he said, taking the bassinet over to the corner.

"I'll go get her changed. Make yourself comfortable. Back in a few."

As she went up the stairs with a flashlight in one hand and Robbie against her other hip, he had to force himself not to stare at her.

He went to the kitchen and popped the last bite of his sandwich into his mouth, then brought the plates to the dishwasher. He put away the peanut butter and jelly and the bread and gave the counter a spritz with her lemon-scented cleaner. Then he brought their glasses to the coffee table and sat down, appreciating the extra warmth from the fire, his gaze going to the photos on her mantel. They were mostly of Robbie, one of Jenna hugely pregnant, and one with her, Robbie and her parents, he assumed, her mother holding the baby.

None of her husband. They were likely too hard to look at, to pass by every day and see him. Diego could understand why she'd keep the one in the nursery, though. That was for Robbie—a photo of her parents.

Diego took a sip of his sparkling water and walked over to the sliding glass doors, the snow coming down fast and furious. He focused on the awful weather to clear his head—until something occurred to him.

There was no way he could drive in this storm—the wind was creating whiteout conditions. And even if it had been the usual Montana snowstorm, he wouldn't want to leave Jenna and Robbie on their own. He wouldn't want a glance out the window to bring on her anxiety. And the lack of power would have him worried about her all night.

That he cared about her was clear. If he could just think of her as a friend… See her as a buddy…

A few minutes later, Jenna was back with Robbie in a pair of cowgirl pj's. She snuggled the baby, pressing a few kisses on her head, then laid her down.

Diego came over and pressed a kiss to his fingertips and then to Robbie's forehead. "Good night, little one. Sweet dreams."

Jenna smiled so warmly at him that his knees actually wobbled. He needed the sofa, pronto.

He sat down and picked up his glass, taking a long sip.

"Diego, I dared a peek outside when I was upstairs. There's no way you can drive home in that." Her gaze moved to the sliding glass doors, which were covered by plastered wet snow. "You can stay here."

He swallowed. He'd figured he wouldn't be going anywhere tonight, but her acknowledgment and the invitation was having some kind of crazy effect on him. He'd be staying at her place. "Are you sure you're comfortable with that?"

"I'm well aware that we hardly know each other," she said, "but I consider myself a pretty good judge of character, and you're a pretty wonderful guy."

He smiled. "Well, thank you. I always keep a go bag in my truck just in case—change of clothes, toiletries so at least I won't have to sleep in my jeans. Oh, and you can rest assured I'm not an axe murderer."

Jenna laughed. "The sofa is yours. I'll take the love seat, since I often curl up on it anyway. Sometimes it's hard to sleep in my bed." Her voice was practically a whisper on that last part. She picked up her glass. "And sometimes I overshare." She sighed, then looked at him.

"Actually that's not true. It's just with you that I seem to say stuff I'd normally keep to myself."

"Ditto. You're very easy to talk to, Jenna Lattimore."

She glanced up at him with those beautiful blue eyes and smiled.

Diego couldn't take *his* eyes off her.

And he was spending the night. In the same room.

Jenna felt so safe and cared for and supported that she barely noticed the snow whipping around out the windows. Granted, it was dark and there were no outside lights to illuminate the rough weather. But she knew a storm was raging, and it wasn't getting to her the way it normally would.

Because of Diego Sanchez. The man sitting on her sofa.

Even the littlest thing, such as discovering he'd cleared the table and put the plates and knives in the dishwasher, had touched her. And how he'd pressed a kiss to her baby's forehead and wished Robbie sweet dreams.

The man had even clipped a perilous branch in her front yard so it wouldn't land on her car—or her and Robbie while they were in the driveway.

When she was a teenager in Bronco, making a list with her best friend about what they wanted in a boyfriend, *a good heart* had topped Jenna's. Her friend's top line was *cute*, followed by *sweet*. She'd married a very cute, very sweet guy, so all had worked out there. Even if Diego wasn't so attractive, that big heart of his would make him gorgeous to Jenna. And minute by minute, he'd shown her just what a caring person he was.

An hour after she'd put Robbie to bed in the bassinet,

the baby had let out a cry in her sleep, and Diego had practically jumped. *Is she okay? Does she need something?*

He *cared*. That was who he was.

And he was so darn good-looking. That face. Once she was looking at him it was very hard to look away. Those dark, dark eyes and long lashes. The short dark hair. And his body. She mentally fanned herself. Tall and muscular with lean hips and broad shoulders. The way his Henley skimmed his chest. More than once she'd found her gaze going to his bronze belt buckle, a cowboy silhouetted on a horse. She really hoped he hadn't noticed.

Even the thought that he might have made her cheeks burn.

She was mentally fanning herself again.

Yes, she liked Diego Sanchez. She just had to accept it. Last Christmas, her mom had told her that one of her wishes for Jenna was that one day, she'd find someone very special, someone who'd make a great father figure for Robbie. When Jenna got back home after spending the holiday in Bronco with her parents, she'd told Mike what her mom said and how surprised Jenna was that she hadn't immediately discounted it. That maybe in a couple of years, she *would* be ready to date again, find that person. Mike had said it was definitely a sign that she was ready, maybe even sooner than she thought. *That* Jenna had discounted. Finding a guy as wonderful as Rob had been? Come on. She'd gotten very lucky the first time around.

But quite possibly, here that special guy was. Early.

And Jenna wanted to know more about him. Personal things.

She took a sip of her water and tried to adopt a casual expression. Like she was just making conversation. They were at opposite ends of the three-seater sofa, facing each other, Jenna's legs tucked up beneath her, Diego's right foot across his left knee. A good distance—not too close, but just close enough. "I guess we're having that date a day early," she said as an opener. Going right for it.

He shook his head. "Nope. The plans for our date included me bringing dinner over and watching a funny show or movie. Spreading jelly on sandwiches doesn't count as bringing you dinner—or making it. And no power means no TV. So..."

So...they were still on for tomorrow night. She had to try very hard to keep a smile from breaking out on her face. She didn't want to seem *that* excited.

But as she looked at him, she thought she saw his expression change for a moment, as though he was thinking hard about something. Second-guessing himself, maybe. Diego was such an upstanding guy that she could see him sticking to their plan for tomorrow even though they were not only having the date impromptu right now—but that it had gotten surprisingly intimate.

The conversation in the kitchen. The hug. How she'd leaned her head on his shoulder.

A chill skittered up her spine—and she recognized it as plain old fear. She was scared of what she was feeling for this man. It might just be interest and attraction and appreciation and red-hot desire, but this wasn't just some crush on a nice and handsome guy who'd done her a solid. A few solids. She was really starting to like Diego. A lot.

Just ask him what you want to know, she told herself.

"So you know that this is my first foray into dating in a very long time," she said. "Since I was nineteen and I'm now twenty-eight. But what about you? When was your last relationship?"

His expression *definitely* changed this time. Impossible to miss. "A long time ago too. I date, but I don't get serious about anyone." Did he pointedly look at her on that last word? Seemed so. It had been *so* long since she'd dated that she was reading into every little thing, trying to get a handle on her emotions. Feel in control.

But that was just it about dating. And romance. And love.

No one was in control. The heart was.

Tonight, the weather was.

Her heart deflated a little and she forced herself to not look toward the windows or sliding glass door, which was completely covered by snow.

She remembered something her father had said over Christmas. *You might never feel ready, sweetie. But your heart will know otherwise and gently nudge you toward letting someone in.*

Right now, because of that comment *I don't get serious about anyone*, her heart was telling her *not* to let this man in. Not to fall for him.

Because when you loved, you lost.

It was hard enough to risk loving *anyone* again. But a man who was telling her he didn't, wouldn't, couldn't commit?

That was a blinking neon warning sign. The red flag of red flags.

Dammit.

She thought about all Mike had told her—and grabbed her glass to chug down some sparkling water.

Pay attention to what he says, Jenna. And heed it.

Except he wasn't saying anything. He seemed a little uncomfortable, and now she felt bad about asking. He'd gotten hurt, that much she knew. He'd said he wasn't what his ex had wanted.

"I'm sorry, Diego. I didn't mean to put you on the spot."

"It's okay. Really." But she had a feeling he was just saying that to let her off the hook. He looked down for a minute. "I mentioned things didn't end well with my last relationship. I was hoping you wouldn't ask about it because I didn't want you to know the truth. But I think it's better that you *do* know."

She sat up a little straighter, intensely curious. "Why?"

"Because we're not a match, Jenna. It's obvious that I'm interested in you—I asked you out, after all. And I'm very attracted to you. But I'm not the guy for you." She felt everything else inside her deflate. She was about to question him when he added, "Can I ask a personal question?"

That was unexpected. "I'm not sure about answering, but you can certainly ask."

"What did your husband do for a living?"

Huh. She wondered why he wanted to know. "Rob was a real estate agent. He loved his job and was good at it."

Diego was nodding slowly.

"Why did you want to know?" she asked.

"It has to do with why I'm not the man for you. And never will be."

She let out a little gasp; she couldn't help it. Never will be? "How? I mean, in what way?"

"I noticed the photo of Rob in the nursery. He was wearing a suit."

She nodded. "Every day. Usually men complain about wearing suits, but he loved putting on a tie every morning."

Again with the slow nodding. "My last serious girlfriend—seven years ago—broke up with me because she didn't think I'd amount to anything. Back then, I was living in the family home, working as a cowboy on the ranch where my parents have been renting a house for years. She said I'd never own my own ranch, that I'd always be just a cowboy."

Just a cowboy? Jenna was still trying to figure out where he was going with the comment about the suit, but the *just* echoed in her head. "What on earth is wrong with being a cowboy? First of all, it's hard work, honest work, and requires brains and brawn in equal measure. And, yeah, I'll say it—there's something about a man in a cowboy hat. On horseback." She smiled, hoping to add a little levity since his expression had gotten so…serious.

"She was right, though. About me. I *still* live in my family home. The same bedroom I had growing up— and I have a roommate, my brother Luca. Like old times. And I'm still just a cowboy, doing the same job I was seven years ago."

Just a cowboy, she thought again, shaking her head. "And?" she asked. "Why shouldn't you be?"

He glanced at her, then leaned his head back against the sofa cushion. "My brother Julian bought land here in Tenacity last month. He's going to get his own ranch up and going. My parents are so proud of him. *I'm* so proud of him."

"That's great for him," she said. "Is that *your* dream? To have your own ranch?"

He shook his head. "No. My dream has always been to be a cowboy, actually. From the time I was four, five years old. I wanted to be just like my dad. I work alongside him." He brightened just a bit. "I've loved that. My father and I have gotten so close over the years."

"That is really wonderful, Diego. And it sounds to me like you're doing exactly what you want to be doing."

"It's not enough, though," he said.

She tilted her head. "For who?"

"For any woman who'd get serious about me. And why would any woman? What can I offer? Yeah, I work hard, I have some money in the bank, but..." He trailed off and leaned forward, running a hand over his face, through his hair. "Take you, for instance. I have no business being on a date with you. A widow with a baby to raise. You need—" He let out a breath and stopped talking.

"A man in a suit?" she offered. Now she understood why he'd brought up what Rob had done for a living. He'd seen the photo in the nursery. Rob in his suit, arm slung around Jenna.

"Yes, exactly. I might work hard and put money away every month, but I also help my parents. And I'll be helping Julian get his ranch off the ground. I'm just a cowboy on a middling ranch, like my ex said seven years ago. What do I have to offer a family? Nothing."

She felt her mouth drop open. "Diego, I didn't fall in love with Rob because of a suit or a job. I fell in love with him when I was nineteen because he was a very good person. Kind, caring, funny. When it rained when we were in college, he'd hold his textbooks over my head. He made me tea when I got colds. He'd go for a morning run and come back with my favorite muffins. He was so happy when I told him I was pregnant, so excited. He was a good man, Diego, and he showed me he loved me every day. I'll choose that over a fancy car any day."

He seemed to be taking all that in. "But you've got a baby to think about, Jenna. You can't date someone who can't provide for the two of you."

She bit her lip. She had an aunt who liked to rattle off that old saying: *It's just as easy to fall in love with a rich man as a poor one.* First of all, Jenna wouldn't know. And yeah, if Diego, the only man she'd been interested in since she'd lost Rob, were rich, that would make life easy. But that lullaby-playing new bouncer she coveted but couldn't afford wasn't a necessity; she had a basic one that Robbie liked fine. And her house might be small, but it had a solid roof and good foundation and everything she needed. Diego got by just like she did and that was how it was. That was absolutely fine with her.

But this was all beside the point because it wasn't like she was planning a future with the man.

A future. Rob Lattimore's face came to mind. She felt a burst of sadness. Rob had considered this house a "starter home" and had said, *One day, we'll have our forever home but* we're *forever, so all's good.*

Oh, Rob.

She wondered what he'd want for her. To not even think about dating for a good five years? Ten?

No. That didn't sound right.

What she did know was that Rob had loved her and had always prioritized her happiness, which had come easy with him by her side.

If I met someone who seemed special, who actually captured my interest, who was sweet and attentive to Robbie, Rob would smile down on me.

He would, she knew. But she was getting way ahead of herself.

And she should be setting Diego Sanchez straight right now, anyway about the person she was.

"I'll always prioritize love and character and kindness over money, over dinner out and a big house. That's what I care about."

She could hear his silent rebuttal. *What you care about and what you need are two different things. And because I care about you, I'm stepping out.*

Not literally, thank heavens. Into the snowstorm.

That she wouldn't be able to handle. And she also knew that because he *was* so caring, he'd never leave her in the middle of a whiteout storm to worry over him getting home safely.

He'd stick it out on the sofa as planned.

"Waah!"

Again Diego practically jumped at Robbie's sudden cry, concern on his handsome face as he looked toward the bassinet in the corner of the room. "Is she okay? What's wrong?"

"She's a baby, that's what." Jenna smiled and extended

her hand to him, surprising herself. Given that Mike's worry about him as someone who wouldn't commit was now proven true from Diego himself, she shouldn't be touching him, which would only make her feel closer to him.

He looked at her in confusion, but took her hand and stood. She led him to the bassinet and gave his hand a squeeze then let go, though she sure had liked how it had felt for those ten seconds.

Robbie was fussing, moving her head, scrunching up her face, kicking her little legs. *"Waah!"*

"I've got you, sweet stuff," she cooed, picking up her daughter and bringing her vertically against her chest as she rubbed Robbie's back. "She's started to sleep through the night last month, but she still wakes up occasionally. Sometimes she goes right back to sleep and other times she needs a little soothing."

Diego nodded and took a step back. He looked out the window at the whipping snow, probably wishing he could leave. Get away from all this intimacy. From the "needy" widowed mother and baby.

But he was stuck here.

Jenna might not have two nickels to rub together, but she did have a voice. And she was going to try to make Diego Sanchez see that he had so much to offer. Himself.

Chapter Six

Once again, saved by the baby. At least that hard conversation had come to a halt. Robbie had gone back to sleep in five minutes and Diego was relieved when Jenna asked him if he wanted a room-temperature cranberry juice from the pantry. And chocolate chip cookies.

He said yes to both, glad coffee wasn't an option. Staying awake all night from a caffeine infusion was a no-go. He'd be mere feet away from Jenna, watching her sleep, itching to push back strands of her red hair from her face, add another blanket to make sure she was warm enough.

And he'd be checking on the baby every ten minutes.

He'd be a wreck come morning and he had to work tomorrow. A whiteout snowstorm might keep him off the roads for several hours, but when the sun rose, he'd need to head out.

They sat at the kitchen table again, both drinking their cranberry juice, a plate of cookies between them. He took one. Home-baked and delicious.

"My uncle Stanley makes amazing chocolate chip cookies. You'll have to try them some time."

She smiled at that. "I think I know who your uncle is.

I saw a couple walking down Central Avenue a couple of weeks ago. Both elderly. The woman wore a purple parka down to her ankles with silver fur on the hood. She was arm in arm with a tall man. I heard a few people calling out hellos to them by name. Stanley and Winona."

Diego laughed. "Yup, that was definitely them. Winona's in her nineties. And they're newlyweds."

Jenna's mouth dropped open, her eyes twinkling. "Really?"

"Yup. Stanley was widowed a few years ago—married sixty years. And Winona had gone through some very tough times. But they met and that was that."

That wasn't that, since they'd both been through hell and back to walk down the aisle. But they'd done it.

"Sometimes, at a family dinner or the other night at the wedding and after-party," Diego said, "I look at them and think anything's possible. A second chance at love when you're eightysomething and ninetysomething."

"So Winona's an older woman?" Jenna asked. She pressed a hand to her heart. "I'm very happy for them. Second chances at love *are* possible, no matter what the prior circumstance. I definitely believe it."

"You're ready to jump in, whole hog?" he asked.

She sipped her tea. "I don't know. I'm ready to stick a *toe* in. It's why I said yes to you."

And here he was, closing a door. Idiot. Jerk. After what she'd been through, after saying yes to even a casual date when it must have been hard, *he'd* said he didn't get serious about women he dated.

But he was a jerk for good reason. It was a fact that he had nothing to offer. Most especially to a widowed mom. A woman who claimed not to care about a man's bank account. And he believed her. But he still wouldn't saddle her with himself. She had a baby to raise. She had to be practical.

They barely knew each other, even if it felt like he'd known her forever. They could go their separate ways in the morning, be friends. He wanted to be there for her, even if she wasn't someone he could date.

Stab to the heart—and twisting.

"Want to play cards by hard hat lamp?" she asked on a laugh. "Crazy Eights? Rummy? Or maybe Scrabble? I know, real exciting. But I do love Scrabble." She looked at him with those warm blue eyes, and it was so hard not to stare at her. Jenna was so beautiful. She'd changed the subject, suggesting something lighthearted to do because she'd clearly seen his expression change.

"I'm terrible at Scrabble," he admitted. "Well, I'm terrible at *spelling*."

Jenna laughed. "Crazy Eights, it is."

"You'll have to remind me how to play. It's been a long time since I've played cards. Like twenty years, maybe."

She faux punched him on the arm. "Lucky for you, I know the rules."

For the next forty-five minutes, they ate cookies and played Crazy Eights, and Diego had to force himself not to lean over and touch her, her face or her hair or even her hand. He wanted to kiss her so badly it physically hurt.

Keep off, he told himself as she dealt the next round of cards.

To take his mind off her pretty face and how her long pink sweater skimmed over her body, her full breasts making him swallow, he glanced at the snow-plastered window, hoping the storm really would stop by 3:00 a.m., as forecasted. Tenacity had a few municipal trucks with snowplows for the roads, but most folks, like Jenna, hired cowboys with pickups rigged with snowplows to clear their driveways before sunrise. He'd be able to get home, to work. He'd never wanted to leave somewhere and stay so badly at the same time.

Diego suddenly realized Jenna was watching him and quickly looked from the window down at the cards in his hand. He could have kicked himself. She didn't need to be reminded of the storm.

"Diego," she said, then clamped her mouth shut.

He looked at her and waited.

She seemed a little shy all of a sudden. "I don't think you know what you've done for me tonight. For the past few hours, I normally would have been a wreck. And this time, because of the whiteout, I wouldn't have been able to get Robbie to Mike so that I could tremble for twenty minutes solo in my car and work it out." She reached a hand to his forearm. "Because of you, I wasn't as affected. I know the storm's out there, but I felt...protected somehow."

He put his cards down and laid his hand atop hers on his arm.

He couldn't take his eyes off her if he wanted to.

She leaned forward. So he leaned forward.

She tilted her head left. He tilted right.

And they both leaned forward some more—until their lips met.

Fireworks. Parade. Magic.

Diego had not been expecting that kind of intense reaction to a simple, short kiss, but maybe he should have.

From the moment he'd laid eyes on Jenna Lattimore, he'd been affected by her.

The kiss lasted all of three seconds. When he opened his eyes, hers were still closed.

"I'm glad that happened," she whispered, looking at him now.

"Me too," he said. "Because I couldn't stop thinking about it. Now I can—" He shut up fast, glad he didn't blurt out what he'd been about to say.

She winced and sat up straight. "Now you can...stop thinking about it because you got it out of your system?"

She sounded hurt. Dammit.

"I... What I said before... I'm not the man for you, Jenna. You and Robbie need someone who can give you the world."

She seemed about to say something, then stopped and got up. She collected the plates and put the two cups on top, then brought them over to the sink. Normally he'd jump up to help, but his entire body felt like a lead weight.

This was complicated. As the saying went, the silence was deafening.

She was loading the dishwasher. She wouldn't be able to run it, but it got the dishes out the way. He tried to make himself useful by gathering the cards and sliding them into the box.

"Jenna, I..." he began, standing up. But she didn't turn around and he sat back down.

Dammit. He didn't even know what he was going to say. He'd screwed up here.

Because Jenna didn't need a man to hurt her feelings

or dangle something in front of her, like the date, and then snatch away any promise from it. He felt terrible.

If she dragged him to the door and literally kicked him out with a sharp kick, he'd understand.

"I'll, uh, go get our blankets and pillows," she said, then practically ran down the hall.

How was he going to fix this when there *was* no fix?

Jenna shut her bedroom door behind her, hit with the chill of the cold air. When she'd first gotten home, she'd closed all the doors, except the bathroom, to reserve the heat from the fireplace. The cold felt good, though. Right now she needed the opposite of a warm hug. She needed reality.

She sucked in a breath, then sat down on her bed, grabbing a throw pillow and holding it against her belly. Reality was exactly what Diego had been saying tonight. *Not the man for you.*

She knew she'd been right about what he'd been about to say—or thinking. *Can stop thinking about kissing you... Got it out of my system...*

Nothing she particularly wanted to hear, but right now, she was focused on the kiss itself.

She'd *kissed* someone.

Another man.

For the first time since she was nineteen.

She'd kissed Diego Sanchez—and she'd liked it.

For a man who'd decided that he couldn't date her because she supposedly needed things he couldn't give her, *he'd* kissed her too. And sorry, Diego, but she wasn't buying what he'd said about being able to stop thinking about it now.

It was a short, sweet kiss, but there was nothing platonic about it. It was no peck on the lips. There was attraction and interest and desire and excitement in everything about the meeting of their lips. That was what the kiss had been about. And Diego had been right there.

There was no taking away that kiss. No backtracking. She knew it. And he did too.

You didn't get someone out of your system by kissing them. That was how you got them *embedded*, actually. One kiss would only make a person want more.

She smiled, but it faded fast. Because she was scared. Excited but scared. No matter what else was going on, Jenna had done something brand-new and brave—she'd accepted a date, she'd kissed a man. She needed to focus on that. Forward motion.

She stood up and went to the mirror above her dresser and leaned forward to peer at her lips. They looked different. *She* looked different.

She looked *hopeful*. Yes, that was how she'd describe her expression, her eyes. Hopeful. That she could do this. That she could be interested in and attracted to another man. That she could go for it.

She could hear Mike Cooper now. *Jenna, he told you he's not the man for you. He told you he has nothing to offer you. Believe him!*

Oh yeah. She knew that was exactly what Mike would say.

The problem was, she didn't want to kiss anyone but Diego.

Oh boy. Diego was probably wondering if she was okay in the cold bedroom, why she was taking so long. She got up and grabbed two down comforters from the top of her closet and two pillows. She went to the door but with her full arms she couldn't open it.

"Hello? Diego?"

She barely got his name out before the door opened, Diego standing there, concern in his dark eyes. He'd probably had his ear against the door, listening for any tearful sounds, worried about her state of mind.

"Are you okay? What happened?" he asked, peering at her.

Oh, Diego. Stop being so there for me.

No, actually don't stop.

"I just couldn't open the door cuz of this," she said, lifting the armload.

He looked at her. She looked at him. Their gazes were locked. There were so many emotions in his eyes, all warring.

If she weren't holding the comforters and pillows, they'd kiss again and she knew it.

"Oh. Here, let me help," he said, taking everything from her.

He turned and headed to the living room. He set the stack on the coffee table while she got two sheets from the linen closet and covered the cushions of the sofa and love seat, then spread a comforter on each and set a pillow at one end.

Jenna smoothed the comforter on the sofa, imagining Diego lying naked under it, not that he'd be naked in her house, for Pete's sake. She wondered what it would feel like to lie with him, snuggled up, spooning, keeping warm, trading body heat.

Kissing more.

His hands on her face, in her hair, on her body...

Okay, she was getting way ahead of herself. For a three-second kiss, it had sure been potent.

"Jenna, I—" he began, sounding hesitant. And worried. Like about whether he'd hurt her feelings.

"It's okay," she said. "We need to be honest with each other. I'd rather hear how you really feel than some sweet words you don't mean. Or worse, now that I think about it, you not saying anything at all."

He studied her for a moment, then finally nodded. "Can I do anything? Check anything? The fire's burning bright."

They both turned to it, the orange flames leaping, the occasional soothing crackle. The living room was warm. Silver lining to a small house.

"I think we're all set. Robbie is fast asleep." She walked over to the bassinet and put the back of her hand to the baby's cheek. Her soft skin wasn't cold at all. She looked at her daughter in her fleece pj's and light cap, her heart overflowing.

Diego was suddenly beside her, looking down at the sleeping baby. "Hope you're having sweet dreams, Robbie."

Jenna smiled at him, wishing she could take his hand and just hold it. Lean her head on his broad shoulder.

But she didn't want to scare the man down the hall and into one of the cold rooms to get away from her and her lips.

She let out an unexpected yawn and realized she was bone-tired.

"I second that," he said. "Long day, long night."

"Thank you for everything, Diego. No matter what, please know that."

No matter what. Even she wasn't sure what exactly she'd meant by that.

He gave her something of a smile, then said, "I'll just go change." He grabbed the go bag he'd braved the storm to get from his pickup a little while ago and disappeared into the bathroom.

He returned five minutes later wearing a long-sleeved T-shirt with *Bronco Summer Family Rodeo* across the front and navy sweats.

Jenna smiled. "I used to go to that every year. I grew up in Bronco. What's your connection?"

"I have family there, an aunt and uncle and cousins. Stanley and Winona split their time between Tenacity and Bronco. Bronco is where they met."

"Small world," she said. "I left Bronco officially right after college when Rob and I moved here. But every summer we went back for the rodeo."

"Maybe we can go this summer," he said, then kind of froze.

She almost smiled. The man was truly in a fight with himself. Saying things he meant but that didn't support his case that they weren't going to be a couple. Yeah, they could go as friends. But…

Summer was the *future.*

"Maybe," she said, giving him the easy out.

He gave her a tight smile and went to the sofa and stretched out. She tried not to stare. He settled the comforter over himself, which helped since she couldn't see his hot body.

Jenna took a last look at Robbie, sleeping peacefully, then curled up on the love seat and pulled the comforter over herself.

This was one of those times that Jenna wished she could go into her bedroom with her cell phone and call her best friend, Mike, or her mom.

She'd kissed someone.

And God help her, she'd *really* liked it.

She must have dozed off because the next thing she knew, she was opening her eyes and felt cold. The comforter was half on the floor. Before she could even move to get it, Diego was lifting the comforter and putting it over her.

He almost jumped when he realized she was awake.

"Something woke me up and I saw that you weren't covered," he said, then visibly swallowed, his eyes locked on hers. He tucked her in, smoothing the overturned top of the comforter. "You can't be comfortable on this love seat. It's too short for a kid, let alone an adult stretching out. I'll switch with you."

She smiled. "Diego, you just said…" She shook her head. He'd twist himself into a pretzel just so she could be comfortable. Without thinking she said, "The sofa is plenty big. We could share. I'm a side sleeper anyway, and you could sack out on your back. We'll conserve body heat."

"Are you sure? I'll be a perfect gentleman, of course."

She suddenly realized what she'd offered, and now it was her turn to swallow. It was one thing to kiss—and a short kiss at that. To imagine his hands roaming all over her. It was another to suddenly be lying on a sofa with him—under a comforter. There was no way their bodies *wouldn't* touch.

That might be just a little too much for her. A little too fast. Spending the night was big in itself.

You must be ready, though, she thought. *To take these steps. After all, you made the offer.*

He'd find an excuse and move to the love seat, she told herself.

Except he wasn't saying anything. He was just looking at her. With warmth in his eyes. And…something else. Something that didn't scare her. In fact, it had the opposite effect.

You are changing before your eyes, she realized. Huh.

"I'm sure," she said.

"Then I am too." He still didn't move, though. Maybe *he* was scared. Of getting that close physically. They'd spent the evening developing quite an emotional connection. Opening up. Sharing. Kissing.

She moved to the sofa and lifted the comforter to welcome him.

Chapter Seven

Diego woke up to the sound of snowplows. The room was dark, but it was comfortably warm despite the fire having gone out at some point in the wee hours. The power must have come back on. He'd get up and go look out the window to see if lights were on in nearby houses, but there was no way he was moving.

Jenna was sleeping on her side facing him, a swath of red hair in her face.

God, she was exquisite. He moved the hair, carefully, trying not to wake her.

"Morning," she whispered, opening her eyes.

Diego usually woke up every morning to a rooster or two crowing and his brother Luca doing push-ups, clapping between them, next to his bed on the other side of the room.

This was much, much better.

"Morning," he said. "Power's back."

"Oh, good! Is that why I'm not freezing?" She eyed the fireplace, just embers.

"Yup. Snowplows are out on the streets. Can't mistake that sound."

Which meant he'd be able to leave soon, within an hour.

He wasn't getting up so fast, though. He liked where he was. And the view of Jenna's lovely face.

He was also rock-hard and if he even turned slightly, she'd feel his erection brush against her. That would not fall under being a perfect gentleman.

And he'd been one all night.

Last night, once she'd lifted the comforter and he'd slipped in beside her, on his back, she'd settled her head on his chest.

"That okay?" she'd whispered.

No, he'd thought. *Not okay. Because something is happening under your head. In the region of my heart.*

You just care about her, he'd reminded himself. *You feel protective. She's a widow with a baby. Her family is over an hour away. And yeah, she has her best friend, Mike, but he's got two jobs and is guardian to his nephew while his sister is away.*

She could use another good friend, he'd thought.

That he could be to Jenna. A friend just needed to be there. To step up. He could and would do that.

Except the word *friend* didn't sound right to him, though. Not where Jenna Lattimore was concerned.

Because he wanted more.

"Of course," he'd whispered back, barely able to speak, as her head snuggled against him, her silky hair trailing on his arm.

Within a few minutes, she was asleep.

Whereas Diego had been wide awake, lying there stock-still. Trying to normalize his heart rate.

It had taken him a while to drift off.

And now, this morning, lying face-to-face... He

wanted her so bad that he was going to have to move anyway.

"Waah! Waah!"

Bless you, Robbie, he thought. Saved by the baby yet again. He owed that little girl.

"I'll go to her," he said, slowly shifting.

"Really?"

He turned to her and nodded. "I'm closer."

He got up and walked over to the bassinet, eyeing the little squirming creature, giving her legs and arms some pumps. She sure wanted out of bed.

"She's seven months today!" Jenna said excitedly, sitting up.

He reached in and carefully picked her up, her big blue eyes locked on his face. He instinctively took off her cap and tossed it on the coffee table. She didn't need it now that the heat was back on. "Happy seven months on earth," he said.

"She's staring so hard at you!" Jenna said on a laugh. "She must like your face."

"Do you?" he asked Robbie, leaning his face closer to her.

She promptly grabbed his nose, then let go and went for his ear.

"That's a good grip," he said. "She might be a champion bull rider one day."

"Oh God, don't say that. Even kidding!"

He laughed. "Sorry."

She got up and came over, standing beside him as she reached up on tiptoe to give Robbie a kiss. "Morning, sunshine. Let's get you out of your fleece pj's finally." She smothered the baby's forehead in kisses.

This is what family life would be like, he suddenly realized. Waking up with a woman you treasured, kissing
your baby's forehead, changing her into fresh clothes.
Making breakfast. Shoveling the porch and steps. Having coffee.

Nice. Very nice. He understood, just last night, why
his brother Julian found it all irresistible.

But Julian had a plan and now he had land, Diego
thought. And he shared a room with his younger brother
in the rented family house he'd lived in his whole life.

"I'll go give her a bath," Jenna said. "Feel free to
make coffee."

As she headed into the bathroom with Robbie, he
went into the kitchen and got the coffee going, then
went to the front door and opened it. The storm door
was still coated with stuck-on snow. He pushed it open
and looked around. The sun wasn't up yet, but it was
nice to see lights back on in houses and streetlamps.
Five, maybe six inches of wet, clumpy snow was on the
ground and in the trees, but the winds had managed
to really whip it around. A plow truck headed up the
street for another pass. And next door, a pickup with a
plow had just cleared that driveway and was now pulling into Jenna's.

He breathed a sigh of relief. He'd leave. He'd wait till
Jenna came back, of course. Say a proper goodbye to
her and Robbie.

For good? he wondered, but the fact that it was a
question told him that was a big no.

He poured a cup of coffee and rooted around the
fridge for the cream, which he figured was fine since
they hadn't opened the door since the power went out. He

took a long drink, then checked his phone. A few texts from his siblings from this morning, checking in that he'd fared okay with the storm. One from his sister Nina:

Happy Valentine's Day. I'll want deets on tonight's date!

He froze.

Valentine's Day.

Date.

Given the storm and all that happened last night, he'd forgotten all about it. Not the date, but the significance of the day.

The bathroom door opened, and Jenna emerged with Robbie wrapped in a pink towel with cat ears. She stood in the kitchen doorway, giving the air a sniff.

"You did make coffee—thanks," she said. "I could sure use a cup."

Diego took out another mug and poured for her.

"Will you hold this cutie while I fix my coffee?" she asked.

The lump in his throat settled in his stomach. "Uh, sure." She passed over Robbie, who smelled like baby shampoo. Robbie's arms were covered by the towel so she couldn't grab his ear this time.

Jenna added cream and a sugar packet to her coffee, then took a sip. "Ah," she said. "Hits the spot."

"It's Valentine's Day," he said—as if he were in a trance.

She tilted her head, then her expression became what he could only describe as wistful. "I'd actually forgotten all about that—more like I blocked it."

"I can understand that," he said. She'd been with her

husband for almost ten years. That was a lot of Valentine's Days to celebrate their love.

"When you and I talked about Thursday," she said, "I didn't realize… But then yesterday, I got a huge reminder at work." She smiled as if recalling something sweet. "When you work in a daycare center, the love holiday is big. So yesterday, I was helping the kiddos make cards for one another and their families and the staff. Lots of hearts and stickers and glitter."

Diego hadn't celebrated Valentine's Day in seven years. His mom had a tradition of making a giant heart-shaped chocolate chip cookie for the family, and Diego always enjoyed his share. But otherwise, he spent Valentine's night catching up on TV.

"That sounds really nice," he said. "I can see the kids now—glitter on their noses, stickers on their fingers. So proud of their sweet cards."

She smiled. "They're all so great, from the toddlers to the school-aged kids that it took me out of my head. But then I got a flash of memory and—" She wrapped her hands around the mug and looked away for a second. "It's my second Valentine's Day as a widow, but I still got sad yesterday while we were working on Valentines. I went to the infant room and held Robbie close and told her that we're each other's Valentine, and I felt okay. Happy even. Plus the fact that she's a *fourteenth* baby takes precedence anyway."

As if Robbie knew her mom was talking about her, a little arm shot out from under the towel and grabbed his nose.

I always did say you had great timing, Robbie. Letting me know while my knees are kinda shaky that I'd bet-

*ter get over myself and give both you and your mommy
a special Valentine's Day.*

He wanted to do something for her. Why not stick
to their plans, even if they'd basically done just that
last night? "Hey, what about our date? I was thinking
of bringing over a pizza from Pete's Pizza. Or maybe
Mexican from Castillo's. I love that place. Their steak
fajitas—so good."

She didn't say anything. She wasn't looking at him,
either. Or Robbie. She seemed a bit lost in thought. She
put her mug down on the counter and held out her arms
to take the baby. He handed Robbie over and she snuggled her daughter against her, resting her head atop the
cat ears.

She still didn't respond.

"Or not," he said fast, feeling his cheeks burning.
"We can play it by ear. If you're up for company again,
great. If not, that's fine. I haven't had Valentine's Day
plans in seven years so…"

She bit her lip. "Oh Diego. I'd give you a great big
hug right now if my arms weren't full."

"Probably better that you don't," he said with too
much emotion in his voice. He stood there, unable to
take his eyes off her. "I could give you a ride to work."

"Oh, that's okay, but thanks. I'm not due in until noon
today. The roads will be perfectly clear by then."

He held her gaze for a moment, then drained the rest
of his coffee. "I'd better get going." He glanced out the
window, still dark. "Cowboy hours—crack of dawn."

She walked over to him and took his hand with her
free one. "Thank you, Diego. From the bottom of my
heart. For everything."

That sounded like goodbye. Which was good, right? He'd told her, after *kissing* her, that he wasn't the man for her. She *should* be saying goodbye, not spending Valentine's Day with him.

He felt like hell. "Anytime," he said, his voice sounding off to him. He ran a finger down the baby's soft cheek. "Happy seven-month birthday," he said to her, then gave Jenna one last smile.

Diego grabbed his bag, got his coat and boots on, and headed out. He shoveled her porch and steps and the path to the driveway, then cleaned off both their vehicles.

Once he was in his pickup, he let out one hell of a breath and started the ignition. But it took him a good few minutes to actually leave, drive off.

He missed Jenna and Robbie the moment he'd walked out the front door.

This couldn't be goodbye.

Mike insisted on picking up Jenna at 11:45 a.m. and driving her to work—not because of the roads, which were all clear now. But because when he'd called to check in with her this morning to see how she'd fared in the storm, she'd told him she'd had company throughout the entire thing. Very good-looking, sexy company. She'd told him all about their night, including the sleeping arrangements in the end. How Diego had—no surprise to her—shoveled her porch and cleaned off her car.

For a moment, there'd been silence. Then: *Well, it was incredibly good of him to follow you home and stay with you during the storm. And help you out the way he did. But I'm not gonna lie, Jenna. I'm worried.*

He was still worried when he arrived in her driveway. Jenna had known Mike a long time and could tell by his expression.

At the moment, though, he was busy getting Robbie into her car seat and playing a round of peekaboo. She wouldn't mention that Diego had done that too.

She watched him entertain her daughter while double-checking that the car seat was properly latched. "You're gonna make some guy a great husband, Mike."

"Don't change the subject," he said, mock narrowing his greenish-gold eyes at her. He double-checked Robbie's harness was buckled correctly, then opened the passenger door for Jenna. Such a gentleman. She was so lucky to have Mike in her life.

"Let's get going and we'll talk," she said. They both got in and buckled up.

"I don't like that he kissed you and then said he wasn't the guy for you. You're a widow on your first date. He shouldn't be playing games."

"I truly don't think he is," Jenna said. "I know he's not. He was pretty open about why he doesn't commit. I told you a little about his past relationship—I guess I just understand where he's coming from."

He ran a hand through his curly brown hair. "Me too. I'm on your side, no matter what. That's all I can really say."

She smiled and touched his arm. "And last night wasn't a date. That's *tonight*." She bit her lip, wondering why she'd said that. She hadn't decided to say yes. Mike was absolutely right about him kissing her and then reiterating that he had nothing to offer her and Robbie.

If he believed that, he should keep his lips to himself, not confuse her and send her mixed signals.

But she had a good feeling that Diego Sanchez was the confused one. That his cautious head and bruised heart were ganging up on him. He liked her—she knew that. He was attracted to her—no doubt. But he was worried that where he was in life meant that he wasn't husband material for a widowed mother.

"So you're gonna let him come over? With dinner and roses?"

"More like pizza and a new toy for Robbie, I'm sure. She's seven months today."

Mike smiled and peered in his rearview mirror even though the car seat was rear-facing. "Happy seven-month birthday, Robbie! I know you're smiling even if I can't see your adorable face."

Jenna laughed. "I like him, Mike. Really like him. But I hear you. And I'm listening. I'll be careful. If he keeps saying we can't be a couple, but keeps asking me out on dates, then I'll know I need to stop this."

"Good. If he hurts you, I'll..."

"I think Diego himself is worried enough about hurting me for all of us," she said as Mike turned onto Central Avenue. They passed the Silver Spur Café and Tenacity Feed and Seed, plenty of folks out and about.

"He really was good with Robbie?" Mike asked.

"Attentive, holding her, playing peekaboo, laughing when she grabbed his nose and ear."

Mike sighed. "Fine. If Robbie likes him, I'll give him a chance. A *cautious* chance."

Jenna smiled. "Good. Because I think I am going to

say yes to tonight. I want to give this a try. Because I do like him so much. I'm going in duly warned by the man himself. But I just have a feeling about him—and that Rob would give me his blessing to take this small step."

Mike pulled into the parking lot for the Little Cowpokes Daycare, then turned to her. "That's really big, Jenna. I'm happy for you. You deserve the world."

She gasped. "That's what Diego said. That Robbie and I deserve the world. It's why he thinks he has nothing to offer us. Because he's 'just a cowboy.'" She shook her head.

"Sounds like Diego has to start accepting himself."

"Maybe I can help. Hey, if I supposedly deserve the world and I want to date him, then…"

"Hopefully he's not too stubborn. You said the ex who'd gutted him was seven years ago? That's a long time. Is he using it as an excuse to not get serious about anyone? Maybe he just can't or won't commit."

Jenna's heart deflated. "Maybe," she said, feeling really crummy all of a sudden.

"Hey," he said, taking her hand. "I'm sorry. I don't have to voice my every worry to you. He sounds like a good guy. He's nice to Robbie. He was there for you, in a very big way, when you needed someone. I'm okay with giving him a chance."

Jenna's heart puffed back up. "Oh, thanks." She gave him a playful sock in the arm. "Seriously, though, I appreciate you, Mike. With all my heart."

He smiled. "Two minutes to noon," he said, gesturing at the dashboard clock. "Better get in there with all those kiddies. Oh, and Happy Valentine's Day, Jenna. I might have skipped saying that to you, but I think you *will* have a happy Valentine's Day."

Jenna did too. Even if her stomach was full of fluttering butterflies.

Chapter Eight

Seven long hours had passed since Diego had left Jenna's house. He sat at the kitchen table of the family home with his brother Julian, both of them breaking off pieces of the big heart-shaped chocolate chip cookie their mom had baked. Once the roads were clear, Julian had stopped by to see if he could help out with snow removal around the house, but Diego and Luca had taken care of that early this morning. After lunch, their dad had gone back to work early to see to an ailing bull, Luca tagging along, and his mom had gone upstairs to put the finishing touches on a dress someone had hired her at the last minute to take in for a special date tonight.

Valentine's Day.

He wondered when he'd hear from Jenna. *If* he'd hear.

"Where you taking Jenna tonight?" Julian asked.

"Honestly, I'm not even sure we're still on."

"Because the plans are up in the air or because you're not sure about dating a widow with a baby?"

Diego frowned. "Both?"

His brother studied him. "I'm just not sure where you're going with this."

Well, neither did he. Diego took a drink of his coffee, and then glanced out the window, nothing but snow-covered evergreens in the distance.

"Oh hell, I might as well just tell you." But he clamped his mouth shut. He wanted advice. He *needed* advice. But he also didn't love the idea of Julian knowing such personal stuff about him. Close as they were.

Julian grinned. "Out with it, bro."

He started with spotting Jenna beside her car on Central Avenue, the snow just starting to come down then. He ended with their awkward conversation about tonight. Valentine's Day.

He mentioned the kiss.

Waking up nose to nose.

And holding Robbie. Twice.

"Okay, that's the equivalent of ten dates in one night," Julian said, slowly shaking his head and then letting out a low whistle.

"Technically, tonight's our first date."

Julian nodded slowly. "Castillo's? Tenacity Inn?"

"I'm thinking the inn. I saw a post on social media that they're having a special Valentine's menu." Usually the inn just served a basic weekday breakfast buffet for their guests. But for holidays they sometimes went all out and turned the event room into a special dining room.

"Sounds good. Plus, if you suggested Castillo's and she said she didn't like Mexican food, you'd have to break up with her."

Diego laughed. "That would solve the problem, though."

"And the problem is that she has a baby?"

"That's part of it. For years now I've felt like I have nothing to offer a woman—and Jenna has a baby to raise. But there's just something special about her." He paused for a moment. "And something feels like it's shifting in me." He shook his head. "I don't know what I'm saying. Just that maybe I've been holding back from committing for the wrong reasons."

Julian clapped him on the back. "Well, duh, *mano*. I mean, I'm trying to picture my life right now if I'd turned away from Ruby and Emery and Jay."

"What was it like, becoming an instant father?" Diego asked, breaking off another piece of cookie and practically crushing it between his fingers. "I mean, I know you and Ruby aren't officially engaged, but you're clearly headed in that direction."

Julian nodded. "All I can say is that it was out of my hands. At least, it felt that way. Those kids had my heart, Diego. As did Ruby. I was powerless." He chuckled. "I laugh but it's true."

Diego nodded. "I care about her—and the baby. But how can I take on a family? It's not like I have any experience. How do I know if I'm even cut out to be a dad? Especially to a little girl who lost hers? And what *do* I have to offer? I'm a cowboy living at home, working someone else's ranch."

"I did for years, Diego. Dad has for years. Being a cowboy, helping your parents by living at home, all good things. But what you need to figure out is if you *want* to take on a family. Because if you don't, you have no business dating Jenna. She's lost too much."

"It's a good thing she hasn't gotten back to me about tonight. She's probably decided it's better that we're just friends." He let out hard breath and dropped his head back. "Jeez, I am gonna die alone."

Julian clamped a hand on his shoulder and smiled. "I don't see that happening. For one, we're having this conversation in the first place. When's the last time you talked to any of us about a woman you're interested in?"

Never.

"Listen, Diego. Your ex was money and status obsessed and said a crappy, hurtful thing. It stung you bad and I get it. But not every woman is like that. You do know that, right? I can name names if I have to. Women you're well familiar with. Starting with Mom."

"It's more that I lived up to what she said I was. 'Just a cowboy on a middling ranch.'"

His brother gaped at him. "You saying what's good enough for Dad isn't good enough for you? He's been happily married for forty years. Raised five good kids and gave us everything we needed by working on this so-called middling ranch. And because you're making me say it, Mom and Dad gave us the most important thing of all—a strong foundation of love, family, commitment, values. Come on, Diego, you know what's important."

Except love and values wouldn't buy Robbie a new stroller when she outgrew hers. Love wouldn't pay for braces. Or her wedding.

Okay, even *he* knew he was getting way ahead of himself.

If he cared about the Lattimore duo this much already, after knowing them a few days… He'd want to give them everything, be the provider they deserved, and he'd fall short.

Julian's phone buzzed. "Ah, gotta head out. Think about what I said, okay?"

Diego nodded but everything he'd heard in the last twenty minutes was all a big jumble in his confused head.

At the door, Julian turned. "You know, hanging on to what your ex said seven years ago gives you an out. You break up with every woman who wants more, a commitment. Maybe what you're really scared of is the love part."

"Scared? Of love? No. Weren't you just talking about the excellent role models we had in that department?"

"So why aren't you married at thirty-three, Diego?"

Diego scowled. He'd just said why. *Because I have nothing to offer...*

It wasn't an excuse. It wasn't.

Diego's phone dinged.

"I'll talk to you later," Julian said, and headed out the door.

Diego was still scowling—until he saw Jenna had texted him.

He grabbed his phone.

Hope we're still on for tonight. Followed by a smiling emoji wearing a cowboy hat.

His frown had most definitely turned upside down.

But then he recalled what Julian had said, about not getting too close to a widowed mom if he didn't intend to get serious about her.

What he *intended* didn't feel entirely in his hands. What had Julian said about being powerless against what was going on inside him? Maybe it was like that.

We are most definitely on, he texted back. I'd like to treat you and the newly turned seven-month-old cutie to the Tenacity Inn's Valentine's Day menu. Pick you up at 6:45?

Three dots appeared and disappeared. She was texting and deleting. For a good fifteen seconds.

Uh-oh. Was she changing her mind? His felt a little pinch in his chest. Disappointment.

Three more dots appeared.

See you then! she texted.

Well, whatever had been going on there, the exclamation point was a good sign.

Diego smiled and tucked his phone in the pocket of his flannel shirt. He popped another piece of cookie in his mouth and finished his coffee. Goose bumps trailed up his arms at the thought of picking up Jenna and taking her out.

He might not be able to answer Julian's questions, but he did know he'd never looked forward to anything more than tonight.

Jenna had made a big decision about tonight. If she was going to date Diego Sanchez, she wanted to get to know him without Robbie as a buffer or as a point of comfort. Or source of conversation. When he'd texted the invitation to include Robbie, she'd been touched, but a one-on-one date felt right.

Mike and his nephew, Cody, were coming over at 6:50 to babysit—and her best friend would meet Diego for the first time. She had no doubt he'd like Diego immediately; it was impossible not to, even if you were very protective of your bestie.

Jenna glanced at her phone on the top of her dresser: 6:38. Butterflies started fluttering around in her belly.

She looked at herself in the full-length mirror in the corner of her bedroom. The past hour, Jenna had spent a little too much time in her closet, trying to figure out just the right outfit for tonight. She'd bypassed her jeans. And her two dresses, one a sundress, the other something appropriate for a wedding. She'd been going for just right—not too dressy and not too casual.

Casual black pants paired with the elegant black mohair sweater her parents had given her this past Christmas—perfect for tonight. She'd added her black leather ankle boots, a delicate gold necklace with a ruby heart to fall in the V-neck, and hoop earrings. A light application of makeup, her hair loose down her back, and a little dab of perfume, and she was ready.

Her first date in almost ten years.

Suddenly, the butterflies started flapping their wings like crazy and she had to sit down on her bed. *You'll be fine*, she told herself. Last night was like a first date on steroids—and it had been impromptu. A planned date... That was a different story because instead of the casual takeout from the Silver Spur Café or Castillo's and some TV, they were going out—on a very romantic holiday.

Diego's handsome face flashed into her mind, and she got excited all over again. *I'm ready in more ways than one*, she reminded herself.

She turned to Robbie, sitting in her bouncer and chewing on her teether. "What do you think, sweets? How do I look?" The baby's gaze went to her mother and she smiled. Jenna decided her daughter was giving a thumbs-up.

She got up and moved over to the bouncer to unbuckle Robbie. Baby in her arms, Jenna headed into the living room to await the ringing of the doorbell. "It's just about showtime." She was equally nervous and excited. "I feel good about this, Robbie." Just as she kissed her daughter's cheek, the doorbell rang.

She sucked in a breath. Gave herself a last once-over in the oval mirror above the console table, and then opened the door.

Her knees actually wobbled.

Diego Sanchez stood on her doorstep. Holding a bouquet of red roses wrapped in beautiful paper in one hand and a bakery box with a tied white ribbon in the other. And wow, did he look amazing. He wore the black overcoat he'd had on when she'd met him in the parking lot of the Tenacity Social Club. The coat was open to reveal a dark gray sweater over black pants. He might not think *they* were a match, but their outfits sure were.

"Come on in," she said. "It's cold tonight."

He stepped in and she closed the door behind him. "You look lovely." She was aware that he was taking her in. That this man who she found so hot was equally attracted to her did wonders for her ego. She'd had a baby seven months ago, and she was soft where she used to be taut.

"Happy Valentine's Day to you, Jenna," he said. "And happy seven-month birthday to you, Robbie." He smiled at the baby and held up the bakery box. "This is for you, Big Cheeks. Just a little something to celebrate your special day." He looked at Jenna. "I'll switch with you," he said. "Flowers and bakery box for Robbie."

"This is so nice," she said, so touched that she had to take a second to let it all sink in.

He gave her the box to start and scooped up Robbie

with one arm, then handed over the flowers. "You won't spit up on my sweater, will you, Robbie?" he asked on a chuckle.

Jenna laughed. "I was worried about that myself on the way from my bedroom to the door. All good."

He hoisted up Robbie and kissed her cheek. "Well, if you do barf all over me, that's okay. That's what babies do."

Robbie grabbed his ear and let out a giggle.

Her favorite sound on earth—her baby's laughter. "I see why she likes you so much."

His smile lit up his handsome face. "It's mutual."

Her heart was thudding so loud she worried he might hear it. "I love red roses so much," she said, taking an inhale of the beautiful flowers. "Thank you. Very thoughtful."

"My pleasure," he said, giving the baby a sway.

"Robbie, let's go put these gorgeous roses in water," she said. "And we can see what's in this delicious-smelling bakery box." There, she was doing it. Using Robbie as a buffer because the moment was…a lot. In a good way, but a lot. If she was going to date, she'd need to get used to all these new feelings.

She was so aware of Diego, holding her child, following her into the kitchen. She had such an urge to turn around and kiss him. For the kind gestures. For making a very sweet fuss. "So, it turns out I uninvited Robbie from our date tonight," she said as she headed to the cabinet under the sink where kept a few vases. "Mike and his nephew are coming over to babysit."

He glanced at the baby. "Well, Robbie, you're definitely not going to miss the Tenacity Inn's steak special, since you only have one tooth."

Jenna laughed and filled a tall glass vase with water, then arranged the roses and set them on the kitchen table. "So true! Robbie, let's open your surprise."

Diego sat down with the baby in his arms, her big blue eyes on the box. Jenna opened it to find three red velvet cupcakes nestled inside. Her hand went straight to her heart. "Oh, Diego, how sweet. Literally too. Thank you."

"You're very welcome. I figure we'll save our cupcakes for dessert later. But maybe Robbie can have some of hers now to celebrate being seven months today."

Her toes tingled. He was basically asking to come back here after dinner. To extend the date.

"Sounds perfect," she said. She went over to the drawer with Robbie's utensils and took out a little yellow plastic fork.

"Oh wait—can't forget this," he added, pulling a little yellow candle and a book of matches from his coat pocket.

Hand to the heart again. Of course he brought a candle and matches. "Look, Robbie, it's a candle!" Jenna said, coming back over to the table. She took a cupcake from the box, then inserted the candle, and lit it. "Make a wish, Robbie."

"My wish is for a big bite of that frosting, Mama!" Diego said in a singsong high-pitched voice.

Jenna laughed. "Oh yeah. That was definitely her wish."

"Time to blow out the candle, Robbie!" Diego said. "One. Two. Threeeee!"

He leaned close and together they blew out the candle.

Jenna had the biggest urge to grab his gorgeous face and kiss him. She was deeply moved. By all of this.

So she quickly picked up the fork and scooped a small bite of frosting and cupcake, and held it to the baby's mouth, which opened wide.

Robbie gobbled it, her eyes lighting up, licking the little smear of frosting beside her lips.

Diego laughed. "I see I made the right choice in flavors."

"Definitely." Jenna gave Robbie one more little bite when the doorbell rang. "That's Mike and his nephew, Cody." She scooped up Robbie and they all headed to the door.

"Hi, Robbie!" Cody said, his brown eyes twinkling. "Hi, Jenna!"

"Hi, yourself," she said. "Mike Cooper and nephew Cody, meet Diego Sanchez."

The three shook hands, Mike giving Diego a serious once-over as he and his nephew stepped inside.

"Thanks for helping Uncle Mike babysit," Jenna said to Cody. "I really appreciate it."

Cody grinned. "I love hanging out with Robbie. She's so cute!"

Cody was such a great kid. Jenna knew he missed his mom while she was overseas. Especially because it was just the two of them—and Uncle Mike.

"Hey, Miss Seven Months," Mike said, leaning over to kiss Robbie on her head.

Jenna smiled. "She just had her very first bite of cupcake to celebrate and no surprise, she loved it. Diego brought it for her."

She had to stop beaming at the man. She could see Mike eyeing her. He missed nothing.

"I was at the Tenacity Social Club a few days back with my family," Diego said to Mike. "I recall seeing you and Cody there."

Mike nodded. "Great place. I moonlight there. My day job is on my family's ranch."

Jenna noticed Diego taking that in. A rancher. *Not just a cowboy.* Maybe she was reading into things, though.

They chatted a bit about the Tenacity Social Club, then the storm last night and how great the Tenacity public works department had been at taking care of business at the crack of dawn. Tenacity might be small and hard-scrabble, but the town had the necessary, if most basic, services. And local cowboys were always on hand with their snow-plow-rigged pick-ups to help out.

"Well, you two go have fun," Mike said. "We'll hold down the fort." There was a slight edge in Mike's voice. A protective edge.

"I really appreciate this," Jenna said, handing Robbie to Mike. "Cody, you're awesome. Robbie loves when you help babysit." She turned to Digeo. "Shall we go?" she asked him, heading to the closet. Of course, when she got her coat, he took it from her and held it as she slipped in her arms. She gave her baby a last kiss on the head, said goodbye to her ace sitters, and she and Diego left.

And then they were in his pickup, driving off toward downtown Tenacity. When Jenna had first moved here, she'd been surprised by how few shops and businesses and restaurants there were. Bronco, where she'd grown up, wasn't a big town by any stretch, but Tenacity had just a grocery store, the Grizzly Bar, Castillo's Mexican restaurant, a lunch place that Jenna loved, not that she could afford to go there more than once a month. The one thing there were two of were feed supply stores due to all the ranches. Tenacity Feed and Seed and Strom and Son Feed and Farm Supply. Tenacity did have one hotel, the Tenacity Inn, where they were headed right now for dinner. And the very special Tenacity Social Club, where teens could hang out after school and on weekends, and nighttime brought open mike performances and folks enjoying a casual night out to have a drink and play some old-fashioned pinball.

"I just love Tenacity," she said, looking out the window as they turned onto Central Avenue. She smiled as she saw at least five men coming out of Tenacity Grocery with various bouquets of flowers.

"Do you?" he asked, glancing at her. "I mean, I do too, but you're from Bronco. I've been there to visit family, and even on their side of town, which isn't the fancy section, there was a lot going on. The town is full of restaurants, shops, bakeries, all kinds of businesses. Winona even has her own psychic shop there. Right on the property of her nephew's ghost tours business. Ghost tours, can you imagine? Tenacity doesn't even have its own movie theater."

"True, but is there better Mexican food in Montana than Castillo's? Yum. We have what we *need* in Tenacity. That's what matters."

"That's true," he said. "That and the wide-open spaces and good people are why I love it too. And I'm happy to hear you like Mexican food. That would be big with my family. But sorry, my uncle Stanley makes the best

Mexican food in Tenacity, though Castillo's is second best. You'll have to come over for dinner sometime."

"I'd love that," she said, that warm, happy feeling spreading in her chest at the invitation.

He pulled into a spot at the inn, couples coming and going. Now she was one of those pairs, out on the town on Valentine's Day when she'd thought she'd be alone for quite a while.

Diego had the passenger-side door open before she could blink. "My lady," he said with a warm smile, extending his arm for her to take.

She was actually doing this, going on a *real* date with Diego Sanchez, scary as that was.

Chapter Nine

Luckily Diego had thought to make a reservation, something that was never required in Tenacity except for holidays. Lots of folks were in the transformed lobby, which was festooned with red garland, twinkling white lights, and dangling paper hearts, some talking about whether they should go to the Grizzly Bar instead of waiting a half hour for a table. As he and Jenna stood in line to check in with the hostess, they read the chalkboard menu on an easel near the entrance to the dining room. Tonight was a limited menu, since it was catered: Filet mignon in peppercorn sauce. Grilled salmon. Heart-shaped pizza with various toppings. Raspberry cheesecake for dessert.

"Mmm, I'm definitely getting the salmon," Jenna said. "And with a side of risotto—my mouth is watering."

"I'm going for the filet mignon and steak fries. I already had a heart-shaped food today so I'll pass on the pizza."

Jenna smiled. "Oh right—you said your mom always bakes a giant heart-shaped cookie for her family. I love that. I want to do something sweet like that for Robbie. Maybe heart-shaped pancakes with red berries. A new family tradition."

Diego could just see toddler and teenaged Robbie enjoying her heart-shaped pancakes every February 14.

They inched closer to the hostess station and finally it was their turn. Diego let the woman know he'd made a reservation, but it would be five minutes until their table was ready.

"Hi, Jenna!"

They both glanced over toward the direction of the voice. A woman he'd seen around town driving a mobile dog grooming van with a funny name—Git Along Little Doggy—sat behind a table on the other side of the hostess stand. A banner hanging down read: *Loyal Companions Animal Rescue Fundraiser.* A yellow lab sat calmly by her side with a harness across his back indicating that he was a service animal.

Diego had noticed in the ads for tonight's dinner that Loyal Companions was sponsoring the dinner as part of their fundraising efforts. Great idea.

"Hi, Renee," Jenna said, smiling at the blond woman. "And hello there, beautiful pooch."

"This is Buddy, my service dog." Renee gave the golden a kiss on the head and got a lick on her cheek in return.

"Aww," Jenna said. "What a sweetheart."

Diego wasn't sure what Renee needed Buddy for, but he knew dogs could be trained to aid people in all sorts of important ways.

"You're fundraising for Loyal Companions?" Jenna asked.

"Yup. It's such a vital resource. Loyal Companions match and provide therapy and service dogs. Such as when someone is diabetic like me and needs a nudge when their blood sugar runs dangerously low. Loyal Companions does such vital work."

"Absolutely," Diego said. "And I'd like to contribute for me and Jenna." He took out his wallet and slipped a twenty dollar bill into the slot on the toolbox, which was decorated with paw prints.

"Thank you," Jenna said to him. "Renee, do you know Diego Sanchez?"

"I've definitely seen you around town, Diego. You have a big family. I know your sisters. I'll be sure and tell them how generous you were to Loyal Companions. Thank you so much. And Buddy here thanks you too."

He smiled. "My pleasure."

"I hope you two will come to the Loyal Companions Fur-Ball next month," Renee said.

You two. He liked the idea of someone assuming they were a couple, that Jenna was his.

As if Renee suddenly realized they might not be at the stage where they made plans a month in advance, she quickly added, "It's a good thing I'm single and have no plans tonight because there's been a ton of foot traffic. I had the right idea setting up here."

A few people stepped up to the table to slip cash into the donation box just as the hostess called out, "Sanchez, party of two."

"Oh, that's us," Jenna said to Renee. "Good luck, tonight. I hope you get lots of donations."

They followed the hostess through the dining room, both of them smiling and waving at several people they knew. Lots of people here tonight, a nice sight to see. Most folks in Tenacity didn't have the kind of disposable income to spend on dinners out, which was why there were few restaurants. But finding it in the budget to celebrate "love day" with a special meal at the inn was clearly important to many.

Diego felt eyes on him and glanced to his left. Uh-oh. A woman he'd dated for a month last summer was glaring at him. She sat a table with a man, and they were both dressed up, but she was paying more attention to Diego than her date.

"Um, Diego," Jenna said once they were seated at a table by a window and the hostess had left. "I couldn't help but notice that Wendy Bean was shooting daggers at you. Even I felt a little scared."

He frowned. "You know Wendy?"

"Well, just from around town. I don't know her personally."

That was a relief. Maybe he should tell Jenna about his breakup with Wendy as a good—and very bad— example of what he'd said last night and this morning. He didn't want to cast a pall over Jenna's Valentine's Day dinner before it had even begun, but being honest about who he was—that was important.

The waitress came by to bring the special menu, take drink orders, and light the short candle at the side of the table, giving him a necessary minute.

He quickly glanced at where Wendy and her date were sitting across the room. They were drinking coffee, then her date left cash on top of the bill and they both got up, the guy helping Wendy with her coat and giving her a kiss before they left. With them gone, Diego felt better about rehashing the story.

"We dated last summer," he said. "For a month. We spent July Fourth together, which happened to be her birthday. But when the fireworks display ended, she seemed to be waiting for something." He frowned again, hating this part.

"Waiting for what?" Jenna asked.

Oh good—the waitress was back with a bread basket for the table and their drinks. Club soda with lime for Diego, since he'd be driving, and a white wine for Jenna. More time to delay telling this story. He rarely thought about it, but when he did, he got a pit in his stomach.

"I wasn't sure at first," he continued. "I'd already given her what I thought was a nice gift—a gift certificate to the yoga studio in a nearby town since she'd been saying she wanted to take up the practice. And flowers and a card. But after a few minutes of staring at me, she seemed really frustrated and upset. She finally said, 'Isn't there something you'd like to ask me?'" Diego took a sip of his club soda.

"Ohhh," Jenna said, making a wincing expression.

"I was confused at first. But then I had that *ohhh* just like you did now. I said, 'I like you a lot but we've only been dating a month and it's way too soon to be thinking about a proposal.' She glared at me much the way she did as we passed by her table and snapped, 'I'm just talking about being exclusive, jerk!'"

"Ohhh," Jenna said again, her voice dropping a register.

Diego nodded. "I did like her a lot. But I'd told her on our first date that I wasn't looking to get serious with anyone, and her response to that was 'Well, you wouldn't be here if that was the case. I mean, why bother dating at all?' I didn't really know how to answer that."

Jenna tilted her head. "It's a good question, though. She likely thought she could change your mind."

Yes. Like many of the women he'd dated. It was a problem he didn't know how to fix.

"Anyhoo," Jenna said, taking a sip of her wine. "How did things end with Wendy?"

He let out a sigh. "I gently reminded her that I'd been honest with her from the start. She stared at me for a few seconds, her expression going from angry to hurt. I felt like such hell. Then she got up and said, 'Thanks for ruining my birthday. Have a nice life without anyone to share it with.' And she stalked off."

"Well, I'm glad she found someone special," Jenna said, eyeing the table where Wendy and her date had been sitting. She took a piece of Italian bread and dipped it in the little dish of infused olive oil. "But tell me this, Diego. Why *do* you date?"

Oh hell. He hadn't expected the conversation to turn to this.

What could he say?

"You're too much of a gentleman to be in it for the sex," she said. "At least I think so. But I guess I don't really know you that well yet."

Dammit.

The waitress returned to take their orders. The steak for Diego and the salmon for Jenna. In those few moments to think, he still hadn't come up with a response for Jenna.

She tilted her head again. "Maybe Wendy, maybe *all* the women you've dated, have been right on both counts—asking why you bother dating and then thinking they can change your mind."

He was confused again. "What do you mean?" He grabbed a piece of bread to have something to do with his hands.

"I think you date because it *is* possible that your mind can be changed about getting serious. You don't strike me as cynical."

Except it had been seven years since he'd stopped dating with an open mind and open heart. He'd call that cynical. But he couldn't bear the thought of shutting a door when it came to Jenna Lattimore. That had to mean something too. Even if his feelings on the subject hadn't changed. "Well, I was just thinking the other day that I didn't want to die alone. So maybe you're right. I don't know, though."

"I guess what I'm really trying to say is that I'm being brave by just being here, Diego. So you should be too."

He smiled. She was absolutely right. But…

"What I said about the kiss and getting the thought of it out of my system? Hardly, Jenna. You've got me turned upside down. In a *good* way. What hasn't changed is my situation. And I don't see it changing in the near future, either. I would never want to make promises I can't keep."

Her mouth dropped open. "All I know is that you've been wonderful to me. Since the second I met you in the parking lot of the Tenacity Social Club. And you just hit the nail on the head—it's not the part about *not* getting serious that needs to change. It's your perception of yourself. And what you have to offer a woman."

Despite how much he liked Jenna, he didn't want to keep talking about this. He took in a breath, the little piece of bread sitting like cement in his stomach.

"Shouldn't we be making first-date small talk?" he asked with a sort of smile.

She laughed and reached over to take his hand. "No. We're well past 'where did you grow up' and 'do you like to travel' and 'who are you rooting for in the Super Bowl.'"

"We definitely are," he said, giving her soft hand a squeeze. He searched her eyes, hoping to see that she was okay with his trying to drop the conversation.

"What I know for sure is that I'm glad I'm here. That *we're* here."

"Me too," he said without hesitation.

"But we can have *second* date conversation, even though technically this is like our third given that our first spanned a second morning."

He grinned. "Agreed. I *do* have questions."

"Oh?" she asked. "Like what?"

"I'm curious about your job. Did you always want to work with kids?"

She nodded. "I majored in early childhood education. I had this dream back in college that I'd be involved with policy somehow, setting standards for preschool, pre-K, that kind of thing. But it wasn't easy to find an entry level job, especially close to Tenacity. My first position was in a preschool as an assistant teacher. I loved it. But I left when I got pregnant, thinking I could take a year off, maybe try to find a work-from-home job part-time. And then Rob died and…"

She stopped talking, her expression tight, and took a sip of her wine.

"And everything changed." He finished for her.

She nodded. "Everything changed. Rob didn't have

life insurance, and we'd put our savings into the down payment for the house, so..." She bit her lip. "I was very lucky to get the job at Little Cowpokes. Especially because I could bring Robbie to work—free childcare is a serious perk. Without that, I don't know what I'd do. The cost of childcare would take my entire paycheck. I've been looking around for tutoring gigs, but they're not easy to come by for young kids."

Diego swallowed around the lump in his throat. He'd been worried about what he could offer when he didn't know she was in financial trouble. Now he felt his shoulders both tense up and then deflate. "That must be a huge weight off your shoulders to have a job where you can bring your daughter."

"It is. Because I can also see her all day. That's worth quite a lot too." She seemed lost in thought for a moment as she sipped her wine. "I love that you achieved your dream. To be a cowboy."

My dream is hardly able to give you and Robbie what you need. That pit in his stomach was back.

"Like your dad," she added.

Like my dad, he repeated silently, the words slamming into his head, his heart. Julian had raised the very point earlier today. Diego was damned proud of his father and held him in the highest regard. Will and Nicole Sanchez raised five children on a ranch hand's and a seamstress's salaries. Yes, times had always been tight, the budget strict. Diego never got the trendy sneakers he'd wanted as a tween and teenager. But even when he'd started working at fifteen and could afford them, he'd given that extra money to his parents to contribute to the household. The family had always had what they needed—and like Jenna had said earlier, having what you needed was what mattered. Birthdays and holidays in the Sanchez household were always wonderful. Did each kid get five presents for Christmas like some of their friends? No. But they all got what was on top of their Santa lists, even if it had be to secondhand.

Diego had no business referring to himself as "just a cowboy" when he was so proud of his father. He had no greater respect for anyone. He'd never really thought about it that way as he'd applied those words to himself in his ex's voice and tone and disdain. His father wasn't "just a cowboy." He was a great man.

Still, when it came to taking on a family in need? A young widow in financial straits with a little baby to raise? That felt like a whole other story.

As if she knew he needed a minute to let her words sink in, she said, "I'll just check in with Mike about Robbie." She pulled out her phone and tapped on the little keyboard, then waited.

He knew from her happy smile that Mike had texted everything was okay.

This what was family life was about. Caring, worrying, loving, checking in, hoping. She was on her own with a baby. Without much money. She had a good support system, including right here in town with Mike, but she was a single parent. That had to be *very* tough. He was about to ask her about that when he realized something had caught her attention across the room.

"Oooh, that's Faith and Amy Hawkins!" Jenna said. "They're sitting with Faith's fiancé, Caleb Strom. You know how much I love the rodeo. The Hawkins Sisters— there are many sets of sisters and cousins—are so amazing. The rodeo stars in their family go back generations. They're so inspiring."

Diego nodded. "Absolutely. I always try to catch a show when they're in Bronco."

"I wonder what they're doing in Tenacity," Jenna said. "Maybe they have family here."

He glanced at the trio. Amy Hawkins was sitting across from the engaged couple, who had turned toward each other for a kiss. Diego caught the wistful expression on Amy's face. Maybe everyone had a complicated relationship when it came to matters of the heart.

The waitress came back with a tray holding their entrées. Mmm, his filet mignon, smothered in peppercorn sauce, smelled so good.

"You should know something about me if we're going to date," Jenna said. "I'm a sharer. So you get the first bite of salmon."

"And you get the first bite of steak. I'll even throw in a steak fry."

They each cut a bite, leaned forward and held out their forks to the other.

It was sort of a romantic, personal gesture, and Diego liked it.

"Oh wow," Jenna said. "So delicious."

"The salmon is too. Thanks for being a sharer."

He was too, clearly. Except when it came to that kicked-around guarded thing beating in his chest.

"Told you so," said a dry voice from behind him.

Diego turned to see Winona coming their way, Uncle Stanley right behind her. Winona was in her trademark purple, a dress with silver fringe, and purple cowboy boots, her long white hair in a braid down one shoulder. Diego stood and Jenna did too.

"Diego!" Stanley said in his happy booming voice. "Nice to see you out on a night such as this!"

It *was* unusual. Diego rarely dated anyone around the holidays up to Valentine's Day to avoid any high expectations. "Winona, Stanley, this is Jenna Lattimore," Diego said. "Jenna, my great-uncle Stanley and his new bride, Winona Cobbs-Sanchez."

"I'm so glad to meet you both," Jenna said. "Congratulations on your marriage."

Stanley's eyes were positively twinkling. He took Jenna's hand with both of his and held it for a second. "Thank you, dear. And very nice to meet you!"

Winona gave Jenna a pleasant enough nod, then turned that stare back on Diego in that Winona way. Not smiling or frowning. Honestly, the woman could be a bit unnerving. He often heard her laughing and telling a funny story to Stanley in the backyard or while they were in the kitchen of the family home. And Stanley had such a big personality that they had to be a great match for them to work so well.

Told you so... Winona's words as she'd approached his table echoed in his head.

"Told me what, Winona?" he asked super casually, smile on his face. Winona *was* psychic. Had she said something cryptic to him at the family after-party at the social club? He couldn't remember. He thought it was his sister Nina who Winona had been talking to. Something in relation to Nina asking Stanley to look up the Deroy family—particularly Nina's first love, Barrett—and see what had become of them.

Winona wrapped her arm around Stanley's. "Have a lovely dinner. We won't keep you."

Guess she wasn't going to answer. *Told you so* could mean a whole bunch of things where Diego was concerned. Something about his date with Jenna, he assumed. But what? *Tell me*, he tried to telepathically communicate to Winona. If she heard him through the airwaves, she didn't let on.

Stanley clapped Diego so hard on the back he almost pitched forward. His uncle was beaming. Diego had no doubt part of that had to do with his grandnephew being out on a date on Valentine's Day. He shot Diego a wink, then the newlyweds left.

"Aww!" Jenna said. "I love them."

Diego smiled. "They do make a great case for second chances."

Jenna's eyes twinkled. "Aha. I was right. You *do* believe in possibilities."

"On a night like this, being here with you, it's hard not to, Jenna."

He almost couldn't believe he'd said it. He meant it. There was definitely *something* happening inside him, something…different. Changing? *That* he wasn't sure of.

Which meant it was time to change the subject yet again. He dipped a steak fry in ketchup. "Can't get these at home. I try to make my own version when it's my turn to cook, but they're either half raw inside or burned. I never get them right."

Jenna smiled. "I make great steak fries. Sweet potato or white."

"Well, *I'll* be the judge of that," he said on a chuckle.

She laughed. "I saw you trying to change the subject,

but look, you fell right into my evil trap of a fourth date. This *is* technically our third."

He felt so much for this warm, funny, smart, beautiful woman that every part of him was pulsating. Including his heart. She deserved a man who wouldn't change the subject from hard topics. And tonight, at least, he was her man. He put his fork down and reached across the table for her hand.

"I couldn't stay away if I wanted to, Jenna. I guess I've dug in my heels about where I am in life. I hate talking about this—especially with you. I don't know how to get my mind around it. Not being able to give you what I'd want. You and Robbie. So then I revert right back to not thinking we *shouldn't* date. And then back to that first thing I said about not being able to stay away. Conundrum. Except I can't and won't play games with you, Jenna."

She stared at him, looking anxious and hopeful at the same time. "Meaning? I'm here, Diego. Do you know how hard I've worked to let go of my fears enough to be here with you? And you're not even going to try?"

He felt that like a punch. But it was still a hard question.

"I'm here. On Valentine's Day. I'm absolutely trying too."

She visibly relaxed. "That's what I thought. But given your past, I shouldn't assume. I'm teasing you a little. But also serious. One day at a time, Diego."

"One day at a time," he said, holding up his glass to her.

They clinked and sipped. Things were okay. Better than okay. They were going to keep dating. What was that saying about necessity being the mother of invention? Diego would have to figure something out if he wanted to give Jenna and Robbie the world.

They were just about done with dinner. Then they'd go back to her house and have those red velvet cupcakes and their date would be over. There was no snowstorm to keep him at her place, though for Jenna's sake he was glad for that. He wanted to prolong the evening. But what could they do that didn't involve taking a walk in the cold, dark February chill? Nearest movie theater was a half hour away, and the show times might not work out anyway. Maybe the Tenacity Social Club? Just didn't seem romantic enough with its dartboards and pinball machines.

And then he remembered something. A poster on the wall at the social club—for a Valentine's Dance at the Tenacity Town Hall. Slow dancing with Jenna? Yes, please.

"If you don't need to get home soon to relieve Mike and Cody," he said, "I thought we might go to the dance at the rec center."

Her face lit up. "I love that idea!" She pulled out her phone to check the time. "I'll just text Mike again to ask."

He watched her tap away.

"We're good to go," she said. "No curfew for us," she added with a laugh. "Cody will conk out early, but the kid sleeps through anything, including being carried out to Mike's truck in the cold and then being transported to his bed."

"I'm like that too. When I'm asleep, a herd of buffalo on the roof wouldn't wake me."

Jenna laughed. "I have Mama radar. I can be in the deepest sleep, but one tiny cry from Robbie and my eyes pop open. I might even hear her while we're at the dance. But I have a feeling I'll be very distracted by my handsome date. Good thing I have a trusted sitter."

Diego smiled. He hoped she wanted to forego coffee to get the dance as soon as possible. Because he couldn't wait another minute to have her in his arms.

Chapter Ten

An eighties new-wave song that Jenna loved, Just Can't Get Enough by Depeche Mode, was playing when they arrived at the rec center, which was pretty crowded. People of all ages—from kids and teens to elderly couples—were on the dance floor. The place had been dolled up for the night and looked so festive. More red garland and many hand-drawn posters of hearts, some clearly done by children and adorable. There was a punch station with cups and many plates of heart-shaped sugar cookies with red sprinkles. Many chairs were dotted around the huge, square, dance area. Jenna spotted several kissing couples. She was so happy that Diego had suggested coming here. It was perfect.

Moonlighting as DJ for the event was the town clerk up on a small stage. A slow song by Beyoncé came on, and Diego took her hand.

"Shall we?" he asked.

"We shall," she said on a giggle.

They found a space on the dance floor and squeezed in, Jenna's arms going around Diego's neck, his hands at her waist, their gazes locked.

Pinch me, I'm dreaming, she thought. This entire

night had been magical. From the cupcake Diego had brought Robbie with the yellow candle to the romantic dinner at the inn and all the honesty in their conversation to meeting his uncle Stanley and his new bride Winona, and now—swaying in a slow dance with a man who made her knees weak.

The song ended but Diego didn't move.

Neither did she.

Another slow one, this one by Tim McGraw, came on. A favorite of Rob's. A song they'd danced to at their wedding. At other weddings. At home.

Jenna froze.

"You okay?" Diego asked, concern in his dark eyes.

"I just, uh, need a minute. Find me by the punch in five minutes, okay?"

He tilted his head, studying her, trying to read her expression.

She fled, heading out of the event room and into the hallway. She leaned against the wall and sucked in a breath, her heart thudding. Tears misting her eyes.

This was all part of the sadness she sometimes felt, and it could strike without warning. The littlest thing could spark a memory of another time and place, when she'd been an entirely different person: a wife, happily married. She wrapped her arms around herself, suddenly cold.

"Jenna?"

She looked up to find Diego's uncle Stanley peering at her with the same concern Diego had a few moment ago.

"Winona's at the dance but asked me to run out to the car and get her shawl," Stanley said. "Is Diego here? Did something happen?"

Jenna couldn't speak for a second. Everything was jumbled.

"I... I was dancing with Diego," she said, her voice quavering. "And another song started. A favorite of my late husband's." She shut up fast, lest she start crying.

Compassion filled his gaze. "Ah, I understand, my dear. When I was first courting Winona, a song, a memory, a movie, the stars in the sky—so much would remind me of my first wife. It was a combination of sadness, unsettling guilt and the knowledge that she'd *want* me to love Winona, to be happy. But sometimes those moments..."

It was so comforting to talk to someone who understood. "This was the first time something so overtly reminded me of him. It wasn't so much that I was in another man's arms on the dance floor. But that I have strong feelings for that man, you know?"

"Losing someone we love so much is unspeakably painful," Stanley said. "Only you can know when you're ready. There's no rushing it."

That made her feel better. She didn't have to go in there and pretend she was fine when she wasn't. She knew she didn't have to do that with Diego.

"You've been a big help, Stanley. Thank you." She took his hand in both of hers.

"Any time you need to talk, you find me."

She smiled, and he headed down the hall toward the exit. What a kind man. Like granduncle, like grand-nephew. She was so grateful that he'd come along when he did.

She looked toward the double doors to the event room, which had been propped open to let air circulate. Winona stood in her purple dress, staring at Jenna from the middle of the crowd. And unless Jenna was imaging it, Winona was giving her a nod. Then she turned and disappeared among the dancers.

Jenna had to smile. Winona, with her psychic gifts, had known Jenna was going through something in that moment, and had sent her husband for her shawl…right in Jenna's path.

Thank you, Winona, she said silently.

Feeling stronger, she headed back to the dance. She weaved through the crowed, easily spotting tall, gorgeous Diego by the refreshments table. Waiting for her. With a cup of punch in each hand.

Warmth spread in her chest. He made her feel safe. Cared for.

He smiled when he spotted her and walked toward her with two cups of punch.

"Just what I need," she said, taking the cup he held out.

"Would you like to leave? Whatever you need, Jenna."

She took a sip of the punch, then another and finished it off. It hit the spot.

He drained his cup too, then tossed them in the trash can.

"I don't want to leave," she said. "I'm okay now. Just had a moment there." She was about to tell him about "running into" his uncle, but decided to keep that sweet interlude to herself. Just like her earlier sadness. There would be times a memory of her marriage would get ahold of her, and she'd feel it and sit with it. She didn't want or need to bring the new man in her life into the thick of that. It felt private in a good way.

"Would you like to sit?" he asked, gesturing at two empty chairs, a rarity at the dance.

"Sure," she said. "I'll just quickly check in with Mike again." She took out her phone and glanced at it. "He hasn't called or texted, which means everything is fine, but I just need to hear him say it. Or see him text it, actually."

She had a feeling Diego knew that her need to hear that her baby girl was okay was tied to what had happened on the dance floor when she'd seized up and run out. That the song had reminded her of her husband. Of a family that had changed in an instant. She'd bet on it.

He gave her a soft smile. "While you do that, I'll round us up two of those heart-shaped sugar cookies with the red sprinkles."

"Perfect," she said. As Diego walked back toward the refreshments table, she sent Mike the text. Song got me all teary but I'm fine. Just checking in. How's my baby girl?

He texted back right away. Sleeping like a champ. Cody played around two hundred rounds of peeka-boo and got the loudest laughter out of Robbie I've ever heard. He also read her five bedtime stories. She was asleep by page two of the first but he kept going in case she woke up.

She so appreciated having a friend who understood that she sorely needed a long, newsy, sweet text.

Aww. Be still my heart. You give that nephew of yours a kiss for me.

I would but he's out cold himself. See you whenever you get home.

Diego came back with two cookies on a small paper plate atop two more cups of punch. He handed her a cup and held out a napkin.

She took a bite of her cookie and so did he, then they sipped the punch.

"All's well with Robbie?" he asked.

She nodded. "Apparently Cody read her five bedtime stories. I have some really wonderful people in my life. Including an eight-year-old." She smiled. "Helps me count my blessings."

He nodded thoughtfully.

She pictured Robbie at home in her bassinet in the nursery, safe and sound, snug as a bug. Yet still... Jenna was here. She supposed she'd have to get used to this now that she was seeing someone. Someone who'd invited Robbie on their date, she reminded herself, brightening a bit, but there would be plenty of times it would be just her and Diego. Like that invitation to come for dinner at his house so that she could see that Stanley's cooking had the edge over Castillo's. She wouldn't bring Robbie, who could neither eat nor talk.

Plus bringing her baby daughter would imply she and Diego were serious. And they were just getting to know each other.

Dating had so many components.

"I'm so used to being with Robbie all the time," she continued. "Except for those twenty minutes here and there when Mike watches her for me. She comes with me to work and then at home. It's just us two. Always has been. It's a little weird to be away from her for so many hours like this."

Jeez, Jenna. A little much all at once. Then again, she

and Diego had been nothing but open and honest all night. Letting themselves be vulnerable. She wasn't going to bounce back from that song and everything it had called up in her in ten minutes. And that was okay. Even when she was on a date.

She could *talk* to Diego. Really talk to him.

"It must be a lot to carry that load alone," he said. "A precious load, nonetheless."

"It is. I've been alone since the first trimester."

She saw him wince. Those days, those early weeks, were hard to call up and reach anymore because of how hard and painful that time had been. Her heart clenched for her parents and Mike, who'd listened to her howl and had held her tight as she'd sobbed, murmuring sweet things, rubbing her back, stroking her hair. They'd made sure she was eating, taking her prenatals, getting sunlight instead of lying shell-shocked under the covers in bed, clutching her blossoming belly. Mike had even been her Lamaze partner, and both he and her mom were in the delivery room.

Blessings.

Diego took both her hands in his. "I wish I could ease some of your worries, but I guess parents never stop worrying."

Jenna smiled. "I only have seven months' experience myself, but I know my folks are always thinking about me. They make that obvious."

"That's nice. Same with mine. And Uncle Stanley."

Again, a warmth spread across her chest. She shifted her hands so that she was holding Diego's. She never wanted to let go.

As if he could sense she was ready to leave, he stood. "How about one more dance and then I get you home?"

"Sounds good," she said in almost a whisper. She looked around to see if Winona and Stanley were still at the dance to say thank you for before, to just be in the midst of their beautiful second-chance love story, but the room was so big and crowded that she didn't spot them.

She and Diego swayed to a vintage Bee Gees song, their bodies so close. She could easily lift up her chin and press her lips to his.

But she'd wait. Until they were home. Or maybe she'd leave that alone. She'd had a big night, lots of emotions going on, and she could probably use some time alone to let it all settle.

A few minutes later, they had on their coats and were headed out to his pickup. The cold air was invigorating. On the drive home, they listened to music, Jenna feeling peaceful.

They arrived at her house, Jenna excited to see her baby. As they headed up the porch steps, Mike came to the door.

"Robbie's still fast asleep. Not a peep out of her all night."

Jenna grinned. "That's great. Imagine if you'd said she'd been fussy and shrieking and feverish. I'd never leave the house again."

"I can understand that," Diego said. "Which is why I'm glad Robbie is sleeping peacefully." He smiled at her, then extended his hand to Mike, who shook it.

Mike seemed to like what Diego had said. So did Jenna. A hint at a future. That there would be another date.

"Well, let me go scoop up my nephew," Mike said.

"I recall that being very easy until he was around four, maybe five. Now, it's like he lifts weights," he added on a chuckle. He went to the love seat, where sweet Cody was stretched out, a throw over him, a chapter book about a robot on the coffee table beside him.

Cody didn't stir, just like Mike had said he wouldn't, even when they all helped his arms into the sleeves of his down jacket and put his Montana Grizzlies hat on his head.

"You're the best, Mike," Jenna said. "Thanks a million."

"Anytime." He smiled, including Diego in it, and he headed out. Diego opened the back passenger door so that Mike could settle Cody in his booster seat. Then the two quickly shook hands again, and Mike was off.

Diego came back, and she shut the door behind him.

With Mike and Cody gone, the house seemed smaller, intimate. As she looked at Diego standing there, his dark eyes on her, she recalled what she'd said about moving more slowly tonight. No kissing? Oh, no, there would *definitely* be more kissing tonight.

"Jenna, I have to confess something," Diego said as he took off his coat and hung it on the rack.

Uh-oh. What was this?

He took her hands, which worried her. "I know we'd made plans to have those red velvet cupcakes when we got back here, but if I eat one more thing, my stomach will literally burst."

Jenna chuckled. Phew. "Same here." Except she suddenly realized that maybe he'd said that to make his getaway—kindly.

"I'd love some coffee, though," he added.

So he intended to stay. She felt goose bumps rise up her spine. "Me too," she whispered.

He bent his head slightly and kissed her.

The sweet passion of his kiss, how his arms wrapped around her, assured her he was exactly where he wanted to be.

Diego was standing by the sliding glass doors to the patio thinking about that kiss when Jenna came back from checking on Robbie. He'd enjoyed the kiss but he wanted more. Much more.

"Sleeping so peacefully as reported," Jenna said. "I'll go make us that coffee."

He swept her back into his arms. "I have another confession." He trailed kisses on Jenna's neck. Her soft skin smelled like flowers.

She leaned back a bit and looked up at him, her blue eyes sparkling. "Oh?"

"I don't want coffee either. I just want you."

Her smile told him everything he needed to know. "Same here," she said just as he captured her mouth again.

He could stay here, in this embrace, forever. How had Diego Sanchez gotten here? Because this woman in his arms had slowly chipped away at the brick he'd built around his heart. Chip, chip, chip. He wasn't sure of anything but that he didn't want this moment to end. And that he wanted a new beginning.

A new chance.

She took his hand and headed for the stairs. At the top, they passed the nursery, then she paused by the door to her bedroom, but kept walking. She went to the next door and inside what looked like a guest room. Diego followed.

Jenna seemed unsure of herself suddenly. She moved over to the windows and nudged the filmy curtains to look out. "I, uh, I...think... I—"

"Honey," he said, walking to the other side of the window to give her some space. He faced her, leaning against the wall with his hip. "It's okay. I completely understand. You don't have to explain or say anything."

He'd known right away in her hesitation to enter her room that she wasn't ready to bring another man into her marital bed. She might never be unless she replaced everything in her room, and it was no longer the bedroom she and her husband had shared, but a new, neutral space.

"Jenna, bypassing your bedroom and taking me in here might be enough of a step for you tonight. A first step about letting someone into your life. No one says we have to rush this."

She gave her head a shake. "Everything about tonight has felt right. *Now* feels right. But yes, in here with this bedroom's lack of personal attachments and memories. The bed is just a bed. Comfy, even for a guest room." She smiled, but he could see she was emotional.

He gently pulled her to him and held her. He pushed aside the curtains and raised the blinds so they could look out at the stars and the moon, not quite a crescent. For a few moments they just stood there.

"Did you pick a star to wish on?" he asked.

She turned to him, surprise lighting her beautiful face. "Actually, yes. How'd you know?"

"Lucky guess. I did too. Made my wish already."

"I want to ask what it was but I won't," she said. "I just hope it comes true."

He did too but he'd leave it at that.

She closed her eyes, then opened them. "Okay, I made mine."

"I hope *yours* comes true."

She smiled and put a hand on either side of his face and kissed him. Tenderly at first. Then very passionately. Her hands were on the buttons of his shirt. Two undone. She was in a hurry, he thought with a smile.

She took his hand and walked him to the bed, then sat down. He sat beside her, the anticipation driving him wild. He'd go at her pace, though, let her run the show.

This was something of a new experience for him too. For the first time in seven years, he'd be with a woman he hadn't run from when she'd laid her expectations on the table.

I'm not here to practice getting back in the swing, Diego.

He'd promised her to try, to keep an open mind, an open heart about the possibilities.

And he was making good on that. One day at a time, like they'd agreed on.

She got up and slowly straddled him, her hands against his chest, and he wondered if she could feel his heart pounding out a beat.

"Just so there's no mistake, Diego Sanchez. I want this. I want *you*."

He didn't need to hear anything else. He laid her down on the bed, inching up her sweater to reveal her creamy soft stomach. His hands traveled upward to her lacy bra. Diego smiled when Jenna impatiently lifted up a bit to yank off her sweater and toss it on the upholstered chair in the corner.

The sight of her satin black bra, her lush breasts filling it, tightened every muscle in his body. His hands found the clasp and he slid the straps from her shoulders and flung it to the chair with her sweater. He couldn't wait for the rest of her clothing to join them.

Diego sucked in a breath as his hands gently caressed her, his mouth trailing over her nipples. Her breathy moans and arching back were making him harder and harder. Her hands found the button of his pants, then the zipper as he did the same with her pants. She worked on his shirt buttons until his own clothes were on the chair, leaving them both in only their underwear.

"Not exactly the sexiest undies you've ever seen," she whispered, her hand protectively moving to her belly. "Baby seven months ago," she added, her voice sounding a bit unsure.

"They *are* the sexiest undies I've ever seen. And you're the sexiest woman, Jenna. If you need proof of what you do to me," he said, "it's right there." He glanced down at the bulge in his boxer briefs.

"I need more proof," she whispered in a seductive voice, slipping her hand under the waistband to his rock-hard erection.

All he could do was groan and throw his head back, focusing on the feel of her cool hand and fighting to keep control.

She wrapped her hand firmly around his throbbing, heated erection and moved it up and down, up and down. He groaned again, wanting their underwear off *now*. She fused her mouth to his, her hands now in his hair, then her nails scraping up his back.

He slowly moved down her body, trailing kisses on her neck, her collarbone, her breasts, the path to her belly button, then used his mouth to nudge away the band of those black panties. She gasped and arched her back as he explored every inch of her softness once her underwear was off. He quickly got rid of his.

"It's gonna kill me to move away from you, but the condom is in my wallet in my pants on the chair," he said.

She smiled. "I love being a femme fatale."

He went to the chair and found his wallet, removing the little square packet. He tore it open and sat down, about to roll it on when Jenna came over.

"I'll take that," she said, kneeling down in front of him.

He almost lost it right there.

She rolled the condom onto his hard length, then inched up to him, very slowly lowering her body on top of him, closing her eyes as they became one. Diego sucked in a breath and gripped the sides of the chair, fighting not to lose control.

She rocked against him, his hands and mouth on her breasts, on her neck.

"Oh, Diego," she moaned, panting, arching her back, her long silky red hair falling behind her. He knew she was close to release. He just had to hold on a few more seconds. A few more seconds as she writhed against him and began to scream, her hand flying to her mouth to muffle the sound.

And then he let go.

She collapsed against his chest, her head on his shoulder, a kiss pressing against his neck.

"That was amazing," she whispered, while catching her breath.

"The best ever," he whispered back.

He shifted and scooped her up and carried her to the bed. They got under the covers, her head on his chest, their hands entwined.

I could stay like this forever, he thought, actually feeling his heart widening, deepening. He cared so much about this woman, he wondered if he was already falling hard for her.

As if in answer, he felt his heart crack wide open.

Chapter Eleven

Jenna woke up in the middle of the night, Diego fast asleep beside her. For a moment, she just lay there, remembering every second of their time on the chair in the corner. When he'd carried her to the bed and they'd snuggled together, she was so sated and spent and overwhelmed—in a good way—that she must have dozed off.

She turned slightly to look at him, this beautiful man with his dark hair that had tickled every inch of her body. Their lovemaking had been passionate and intense and full of promise. She'd felt his intentions in every kiss, every thrust. In the way he'd held her close afterward, kissing her cheek, her forehead. The tenderness almost made her cry.

That was when the trouble had started for her.

She bit her lip and turned to face away from him, needing to figure out what she was feeling, what was happening in her head, in her heart.

It was too much, too soon. She understood that. The passion, fine. The passion combined with the tenderness? Way too much.

I can't fall in love with him, she thought, tears misting her eyes. *I can't love someone else.*

And not because of Rob. Not because of guilt.

Because of *sorrow*. Of heartbreak so painful and wrenching she couldn't bear the thought of going through it again.

She'd loved with all her being and had lost hard. She could see herself falling in love with Diego and living in constant fear and worry every time he drove off in his pickup no matter the weather conditions. Every time he was out on the range on a steep ledge with the cattle. Every time he rode a horse.

I can't do this, she thought, a familiar panicky feeling echoing those words in her head.

She quietly slipped out of bed, piled Diego's clothes neatly on the chair, then collected her own and hurried from the room, closing the door behind her. When she entered her bedroom, the bedroom where she and Rob had made love endlessly, where they'd watched late night TV and movies afterward in bed. Where Rob munched on his favorite snack of red grapes and she knitted after a long day. She flashed back to their last night together, when she'd been working on yellow baby booties because she'd found out just a few days prior that she was expecting.

Rob had been beside himself with happiness.

The next day, he was gone.

Because that was how life was. It changed in an instant.

Like when she met Diego Sanchez in the parking lot of the Tenacity Social Club. Her whole life had changed with that tap on her car window, leading to that chair in her guest room.

She felt so much for him—to the point that he was able to even get in the guest room.

She closed her eyes and dropped down on her bed, staring out the window at the inky night, at the same stars she and Diego had looked at in the room next door just hours ago, each choosing a star and making a wish.

Her wish? That this wasn't a dream, that he'd change his mind about what he had to offer, that he'd be all in.

She'd dashed her own dream without even giving him a chance.

Tears stung her eyes again and she got up and went into the bathroom, her gaze falling on the baby monitor sitting on the counter. She moved to the shower and turned on the water. Part of her wanted to keep every imprint of his lips, every scent from their lovemaking on her. But a bigger part needed to wash it all away.

Her heart aching and heavy, she stepped under the hot spray of water, soaped up her body and hair, and cried hard.

When she emerged, wrapping a thick towel around her, another for her hair, her feet in her soft slippers, she felt much better. She wasn't scared anymore because she'd settled on a decision about Diego. They could be friends. Good friends. He'd understand, surely.

You should have come to this before you slept with him, she chastised herself.

Her heart clenched at that. She should have. But she wouldn't have gotten to this point, of understanding that she could not handle loving him, without having been brought to the brink of it.

I'm sorry, Diego, she thought sadly, facing herself in the mirror. She dried off her hair and tied it back into a ponytail, then got dressed in a long pale pink sweatshirt and gray yoga pants. She changed her slippers for fuzzy warm socks. She looked at herself long and hard in the mirror. Self-preservation, she told herself.

She stared at the baby monitor. Aside from being unwilling to experience the pain she'd suffered when she lost Rob Lattimore, a great man who'd never gotten the chance to meet his child, she needed to be a very present mother. She was worried enough about her financial situation without adding being a panicked mess every time Diego left her side. Robbie didn't need her sole parent to be distracted like that. She'd made promises to Robbie about being a good mother. And she'd keep them.

Jenna let out a deep breath and went to Robbie's nursery. Standing over her daughter's bassinet, she felt her resolve strengthen. Yes, this was what was most important. This baby. She pressed a fingertip to her lips and then to Robbie's soft auburn wisps.

Then Jenna curled up in the glider chair by the window, moving the cozy throw over her, and closed her eyes.

Diego woke with a smile on his face, his eyes still closed. Mmm, the memory of making love to Jenna was so fresh that he could replay it without missing one delicious thing. He opened his eyes, not wanting to wait another second before seeing Jenna's beautiful face.

Or to tell her that he was in this 100 percent. He understood now, because of Jenna herself, that his ex had been one woman with a particular mindset. No, he couldn't give *that* woman what she wanted or needed. What he wished he'd understood in hindsight was that he shouldn't want to give anything of himself to a woman who valued a job title and a bank balance over deep and abiding love.

His family had tried to tell him, but he'd shut everyone out on that subject. Shamed and bruised and battered.

Not anymore. Because of the depth of his feelings for Jenna, she'd gotten through. Julian's wise words yesterday about their dad had gotten through.

He got it now. He might not be able to buy out the baby department of a big box store, but he could provide for Jenna and Robbie. He finally understood that that was enough. That he was good enough, as he was.

Thank you, Jenna Lattimore.

He turned, but Jenna wasn't in bed with him. Her clothes were gone from the chair, his own stacked neatly.

The sun wasn't quite up yet so it was very early. He hadn't heard Robbie cry, but Jenna clearly had. He couldn't wait to see her, wrap her in his arms, hold that precious little baby to his chest. This was all just beginning, but he was ready for it. Ready to be what Jenna needed: a man she could trust, count on, who could support her and Robbie in all ways, including financially, though granted, not with a new car every few years like folks seem to have in Bronco Heights or vacations beyond camping every summer. Anyway, he could easily pick up an extra hour a day on the ranch and let a rainy-day fund grow. A family fund.

He quickly dressed and went in search of Jenna. She wasn't in the nursery. And the crib was empty too, so they must be downstairs. He rushed down, his heart practically bursting with how much he had to tell her.

He heard her talking to Robbie in the kitchen.

"We're gonna visit Grandma and Grandpa today in Bronco," she was saying. "They're gonna be so surprised and happy to see you, Robbie!"

He paused. Bronco. Three hours round trip. Then two to three hours there. She'd be gone all day. And it was clearly an impromptu visit—to get away. Or she would have mentioned it last night.

She stopped talking when he entered the room, her expression going from animated to...

Serious. Worried. Sad.

And she wasn't saying anything, like *Good morning* or *I had a great night's sleep* because of all that strenuous activity or coming over to kiss him and wrap her arms around him.

The way he wanted to do to her.

But he was immediately aware that he shouldn't. That something had changed.

His heart sank with the realization that not only had something changed, but that something was very wrong.

He wasn't going to put her on the spot. Not with Robbie in the high chair, enjoying the mashed banana Jenna was feeding her with a spoon.

"Morning," he said, attempting a slight smile. He wasn't successful.

She glanced at him, that strange expression still on her beautiful face, then back at Robbie. "Morning."

Give her the time she needs, he told himself. It was all he could do now.

"Wish I could stick around this morning," he said to let her know at least that, "but I need to hit the road, get to the ranch. Can I make you a cup of coffee before

I go?" He wished he could tell her what last night had meant to him. What she and Robbie meant to him. But this wasn't the time.

Her expression remained strained. If she said yes to coffee, he'd know she wanted him to stay a bit. If she said "No, I had a cup already," he'd know she wanted him to leave right now. And that he was correct about the way she was feeling. Differently from last night, that was for sure.

"No, thanks," she said, his heart sinking. "I already had a cup. Robbie woke even earlier than usual. All that good sleeping through the night last night."

He managed a smile at Robbie. "I'll get going then. Talk tonight?"

She was pushing the spoon into the banana and mashing it a bit. "Yes. Definitely."

He nodded and turned to go.

"Diego?" she called.

His heart lifted and he turned around.

"I… I just…" She bit her lip and stopped talking. She looked like a woman who didn't want to tell the man she'd just slept with that she was sorry but she couldn't do this after all.

Which dammit, he understood. She had every right to take this as it came, see how she felt. Sometimes you didn't know how you felt until you went too far. But what they had was so…special.

"Jenna, it's okay. No worries. No matter what, I care about you and Robbie. That'll never change, no matter what we are to each other."

It was true, but it stung. Because he'd just come around. In the other direction than she went.

She stood and put down the spoon and walked over to him, her expression a mixture of sad and resolute. "You're a wonderful person, Diego Sanchez. And I'm lucky to know you."

That sounded like goodbye. His chest tightened, his shoulders tensed. He wanted to fight for her but now was not the time. Not with Robbie having her breakfast. Not with Jenna needing some space between them. *Put her first*, he told himself.

"Ditto," he said, and gave her a fast hug back, relishing the feel and scent of her. Then he let go and turned again, heading to the coatrack. He needed air and some time to let this settle.

But dammit, it hurt.

The moment Jenna turned onto her parents' street, she relaxed. She hadn't lived in Bronco in ten years, but the sight of the house she'd grown up in, the familiar brick Cape with its welcoming red door and black shutters, did a weary heart good.

She knew that Diego had relatives in town, in Bronco Valley, the less affluent side of town where she grew up. Her mother was a longtime happy customer of hairstylist Denise Sanchez, who managed a salon nearby. Jenna was pretty sure Denise and her husband, Aaron, were Diego's aunt and uncle. It was a small world.

She couldn't stop thinking of the Sanchez in *her* life. His face when he'd stood in the doorway of the kitchen that morning. She'd had a script in her head for what to say, to avoid any real conversation in the moment with Robbie right there, eating her mashed banana. They'd talk later, she'd figured. But she'd been able to tell that he knew something had changed between the time they'd fallen asleep naked in each other's arms and when he'd awoken.

She felt terrible about it. And because Diego put others before himself, he'd understood and had quietly left.

Her heart still hurt.

As she was taking Robbie out of her car seat, her parents came out all bundled up. Her parents each hugged her, then her dad said he was taking his grandbaby to the nursery to put on a puppet show—they'd found an adorable little stage and puppets at a thrift sore—and to read her stories.

Code for: *so you and Mom can talk.*

They knew that Jenna didn't make impromptu midweek visits, an hour and a half away, unless she was needing her mom's advice and her dad's hugs and hot chocolate.

Inside, her dad got Robbie out of her snowsuit. "Give Mama a kiss before we go to the puppet show by yours truly."

Jenna kissed her daughter's baby-shampoo-scented head. "Enjoy the show, sweetie. And thanks, Dad."

Her father winked at her and headed upstairs. The house had three bedrooms, and they'd turned a guest room into a nursery with everything Robbie needed while they were visiting. Her dad had been able to pick up everything secondhand.

She and her mother smiled as her father chatted to Robbie the entire trip up the stairs. Her parents were the best.

"Difficult night?" her mom asked, voice full of compassion as they walked into the living room. Her mom knew all about difficult nights. Her parents had stayed with her for six weeks after she'd lost Rob; they'd been in the thick of it. In the months after, her mother would call every night, and sometimes Jenna was managing and sometimes she'd be unable to stop crying.

Jenna sank down on the sofa, her mother sitting beside her. "Didn't start out that way. I make the mistake of thinking I could actually start seeing someone. A very handsome, very kind cowboy named Diego."

Her mom's eyes widened. "What happened? You were honest about your needs and he couldn't handle it?"

"Oh, he could, actually. He could handle anything. The problem turned out to be me."

She told her mom everything, including that they'd spent the night together, two nights, but how *last* night, Jenna had given into her attraction and feelings. Until she'd woken up in the middle of the night.

Choking. Seized up. Scared.

Her mom took her hand and held it. "I know it's a cliché to say, but all love comes with risk, Jenna."

"I know that. It's why I'm backing out. Why I can't keeping seeing Diego. How can I let myself fall in love with someone when *anything* can happen? I have enough people in my life to worry about on a daily basis."

"I understand, sweetie. Of course I do. What I think you're really saying is that you're just not ready."

Jenna wasn't sure that was really the issue. "How can I ever be ready to fall for someone I could lose, though?"

"I wish I had words of wisdom for you. All I know is that this man must be pretty special for you to have gotten involved with him in the first place."

"He is," she said, trying to blink Diego's image from

her mind. That face. The kindness. Memories of their night together.

She missed him so much already. How was she going to cut him out of her life?

They'd be friends. But how did you go from an intense attraction and deep interest to being platonic? How did you just shut off the romance, the sexual desire?

Maybe it would be easier than she thought. Because her fear seemed to trump everything else.

"Let's go bake something gooey and fattening," her mom said. "And eat every bit of it."

Jenna smiled. "Good idea."

But then her smile faded as she was reminded of Diego saying he had to pass on the red velvet cupcakes because he was bursting at the seams from dinner and the cookies at the dance. How nervous she'd been that he was making an excuse not to stay for their planned dessert. How thrilled she'd been when he'd asked for coffee.

All leading to a night she'd never forget as long as she lived. The passion, the tenderness.

She followed her mother to the kitchen, where she'd baked by her mom's side from the time she was three years old. The cheery room with the same white round table, the same wallpaper with its leaf motif, was so comforting that Jenna instantly felt better.

"All you can do is what feels right," her mom said as she started setting out the ingredients for Jenna's favorite cake: good old chocolate layer. "Whether that's spending the night with Diego or backing away because you're scared or anywhere between those two. Nothing you feel is wrong, Jenna. Just know that."

Jenna squeezed her mom's hand. "Thanks. Just what I needed to hear."

And it really was. A relief since following her heart, her head was all she *could* do.

Chapter Twelve

All morning at work, while Diego herded cattle to a different snowy pasture, while he'd checked over a Black Angus heifer that had been acting off, while he'd helped out the hands with a feed delivery that needed unloading, he'd been asked the same question: *You okay?*

He wasn't okay and wasn't surprised his emotions showed on his face. This morning had been rough. To the point that he barely felt the cold Montana wind whipping at his cowboy hat and trying to get through his leather barn coat and work gloves. It wasn't just the big change in Jenna from last night to this morning—especially right after he'd had a big change happening inside himself and in the opposite direction. But that he couldn't talk to her about it. Not till she got back from Bronco. He couldn't call or text her while she was visiting with her folks, and he certainly wouldn't interrupt her on a long drive. He'd just have to wait to hear what she had to say.

He'd had the same response for everyone who'd taken one look at his grim face and asked if he was okay—his dad, a few fellow cowboys, even the foreman. Two other cowboys had mentioned they'd seen him at the dance getting up close and personal with a pretty redhead—was she his new girlfriend?

Diego had answered honestly, which had surprised him: "I don't know but I hope so."

He'd never thought such a line would come out of his mouth, but there it was. Things could and did change. People could change.

Unfortunately, that didn't mean anyone else was in the same mindset at the same time.

He'd gotten tipped hats and claps on the back, which made him feel worse, since by tonight, it would be official that they weren't a couple.

And now, just past 1:00 p.m., he was keyed up and tense and needed to get out of here. Off the ranch. A change of scenery would do him good. He didn't have much of an appetite, but he could use coffee.

He got in his truck and headed into town, parking by the Silver Spur Café. As he was getting in line to order at the counter, he noticed a very familiar long dark ponytail right in front of him.

"Hey, Nina," he said.

His sister turned with a surprised smile. "You're here? You never come here."

His shrug must have been extra pathetic because she peered at him closely.

"Something's wrong," she said, studying him. "Is Dad okay? Mom? Luca?"

"Everyone's fine," he assured her.

"Except you." It was her turn to order. "What are you having?" she asked him.

"Large regular coffee," he told the waitress.

He was so distracted he hadn't even noticed Nina had

gotten herself a coffee too and paid for them both. He'd get it next time. "Thanks."

They moved over by the window, which had a bar and stools.

"I'll assume this has something to do with Jenna Lattimore," she said, sipping her coffee.

Oh hell, he might as well tell her. He needed to talk to someone, and Nina was a good listener and always gave solid advice. "Just when I came around to taking things to the next level—"

Her mouth dropped open. "Wait, the next *level*? You're thinking of proposing?"

"The next level for me is an actual relationship beyond a few dates."

"I should have known. Sorry—continue. Just when you came around, she…"

"Changed her mind," he said. "I'm sure it has to do with her actually taking that next step herself and then getting cold feet. She and her husband were together since she was nineteen. He died just over a year ago."

"Must be very hard," Nina said compassionately. "She's also raising a baby on her own."

He nodded, picturing Jenna holding Robbie, snuggling her close. "I want to be there for her, take care of her—*them*. If she just wants to be friends, fine, I'll be the best friend she's ever had, though she has one of those already. But…" He let out a hard breath and hung his head back.

"But you have serious feelings for Jenna. And the baby."

He nodded again, that adorable little girl coming to mind with her big blue eyes and penchant for grabbing his nose and ear. "Robbie. She's so cute. Turns out I like holding a baby."

Nina was staring at him, wonder in her expression. "Wow, you have really done a one-eighty, Diego."

He really had. "I guess Julian was right. It just comes for you and that's that."

"By 'it' do you mean love?" She grinned but then looked at him thoughtfully.

Love. Was that what this was? Maybe. Love was a *big* word. He shrugged. "I just know that I've never felt this way before," he said.

She grabbed his hand and gave it a squeeze. "I'm so damned happy to hear that. And I think things will work out just fine. But right now, Jenna's going through some huge changes. Scary changes."

Scary changes. Like caring about someone else again.

"I know," he said. "I just hope she doesn't shut me out. I want to help. Without putting any pressure on her."

"She probably just needs time. For you, everything is brand-new. But for her, it isn't—and the last time she did this, she lost everything in the most painful way possible. She's going to react, she's going to freak out, she's going to retreat, but she'll likely come running too. Just let her do what she needs to—and when."

He nodded, taking all that in. "I will." He slugged down his coffee, the caffeine boost and Nina's excellent advice buoying him. "I owe you, *mana*. For the coffee and the sisterly wisdom."

"Anytime," she said with a smile. Her phone buzzed and she glanced at it. "Gotta run. Let me know how it goes. I like details."

"Will do," he said. "Though maybe not the details."

She squeezed his hand and left. Diego sat for a few more minutes, finishing his coffee. He checked his own phone as though there would magically be a text when there was no notification.

There wasn't.

He wanted to hear from Jenna so badly. But at least when they talked tonight, he'd be a bit more grounded. It had helped to talk it all out with Nina.

Would Jenna come running? He wasn't so sure of that. Come inching toward him? Maybe. But it opened the possibility that he had a shot at keeping her in his life.

Jenna couldn't relax. She was pacing around the living room, clasping and unclasping her hands, straightening perfectly straight photo frames and candlesticks on the mantel.

Diego would be here any minute.

She'd texted him right before she'd left her parents' house a few hours ago.

Can we talk tonight? After Robbie's bedtime at 8:30?

He'd texted back in three seconds. I'll see you then.

She was not looking forward to this conversation. But she *was* looking forward to seeing him. For what might be the last time.

She bit her lip and rearranged the order of the items on the coffee table, then put them back the way there were. It would be just her and Diego. Robbie was asleep in the nursery, so there would be no stalling to put her to bed, no buffer of small talk over how Robbie had fallen asleep early or how cute the new Valentine-themed footie pajamas were that her parents had insisted on buying for their granddaughter during a trip into town.

Jenna heard the pickup truck pulling into the driveway and her heart rate sped up even though she knew exactly how this would go. She would tell him how she felt. He would tell her it was okay, he understood, no worries. He'd give her a hug. That was Diego. And it wasn't fair that someone so supportive was being treated this way. After that beautiful night together.

She closed her eyes for a second, not used to feeling like a heel. *I'm sorry, Diego.*

While she and her parents had been at Sadie's Holiday House, a gift shop in Bronco, something had occurred to her: that Diego might actually be relieved. He was at the "trying" stage, going from his usual casual dating to keeping an open mind about a real relationship between them. Perhaps he'd feel a weight off his shoulders, a pressure gone when she told him she couldn't do this after all. They had gotten to a point where he had to be feeling uncomfortable. Especially because they'd slept together.

She remembered his face this morning, his expression when it was clear that something had changed for her. It was the look of a relieved confirmed bachelor.

Her phone pinged with a text. I'm here. Didn't want to ring the bell and wake Robbie.

That was Diego Sanchez. Summed up right there in the tiniest gesture why she'd felt so safe, so cared for, so supported that she'd slept with him.

And the moment she opened the door and saw him, she remembered the other part of why she'd taken him into the guest room. That handsome face. His deep brown eyes. The tall, muscular body. She had to suck in a breath at his effect on her. How she wanted to grab him to her and kiss the living daylights out of him.

But a second later, she envisioned him on a horse near a steep drop. Behind the wheel of a car on a slick road. Just going about his daily life when anything could happen, anytime. Rain or shine.

And her resolve strengthened. That she was intensely attracted to him and had very strong feelings were not in question.

Nor was her ability to deal with loving and losing all over again.

Because it was out of the question. She'd done a lot of thinking on the long drive back from her parents' house and she'd come to some important realizations. She'd share them with him tonight.

"How was the drive there and back?" he asked. "Any traffic?"

"Not at all," she said, shutting the door behind him and leading the way to the living room. Neither of them sat, though. Jenna stood kind of awkwardly by the fireplace, and Diego was beside the sofa. "I made good time and I *had* a good time. Seeing my parents was just what I needed. And they doted on their grandbaby, of course."

"I'm sure," he said with a half smile. Then he looked at her intently. "Jenna, I want to tell you something. Whatever you're feeling, whatever you need to say to me or do, it's okay. I understand. Whatever you need from me, that's what I'll be. But… I just don't want something to get lost or unsaid, so here goes."

With everything in her she had to fight the urge to close the few feet between them and throw her arms around him. Hold on for dear life. Because it didn't work that way. There *was* no holding on.

She'd learned that the hardest way possible.

"I want this," he continued. "*Us.* I want to be with you. I want to be there for Robbie in whatever way you feel comfortable with. I'm in this one hundred percent. There's no more trying. There's no need to try. I'm *there*, Jenna."

Oh, Diego. Her heart squeezed so tightly that she had to press her hand to her chest. He *wasn't* going to be relieved to hear what she had to say.

"I won't speak for you," he said. "But I think I understand what happened between the time we dozed off and this morning. Or the middle of the night when you left the bed."

He paused for a moment, looking away and then back at her. Her heart went out to him—at how hard he was fighting for this. For them. At how much he *had* changed.

There's no more trying... I'm there...

This wasn't fair to him at all. And she couldn't do anything about it.

"You lost your husband, your partner of almost ten years," he continued. "And now you're involved with me and it's calling up all those scary, painful feelings. You don't want to go through anything like that again."

That was exactly right. It almost helped to hear him say it.

"I *can't*," she said. "I realized something on the ride home from Bronco. That I'm finally in an okay place. It's why I was able to be romantically involved with you in the first place, to sleep with you. In those early months after I lost Rob I was a wreck who sobbed constantly and needed to hold my infant daughter to get through the day. I'm okay now, Diego, except for the occasional time when I need a half hour to sit with it. And I want to leave that alone, leave myself in peace. For me and for Robbie."

He seemed to be taking that in and was quiet for a moment. "I'm not going to stand here and try to convince you to let me in, Jenna. I refuse to pressure you. You have every right to your feelings. I won't lie—I want to fight for you. But the cowboy code has a clause about that."

She managed to smile through the tears suddenly stinging her eyes. "I'll keep being honest here. All I want right now is for you to hold me. I need you, Diego. But *you're* the one I'm in danger from. How did everything get so upside down?" The tears started falling, and she wiped them away.

"Well, there's where I'll tell you you're wrong," he said, stepping toward her. "I'm not the danger. The fear is coming from here." He reached out his hand and pressed it to her heart. "I know what you mean, though. I'm scary. What we have is scary. And loss is heart-wrenching. Jenna, this is beside the point right now, but *you're* scary as hell to *me*. Because of how I feel about you."

She flew to him then, wrapping her arms around him. He held her tightly as she cried. "I do need you, Diego. I need you, but I can't have you in my life." She wasn't letting go, though. She couldn't seem to do that, either.

"I have an idea," he said gently. "What if we take this so slowly that you don't even know there's an us?"

She leaned her head back and looked at him, her expression brightening just a bit. "What do you mean?"

"What if we just go minute by minute, Jenna? At the core, we have a beautiful, necessary friendship. If you want more in any given moment, any given day, great. If not, absolutely fine. We go at your pace so you can get used to dating, to letting yourself care about someone again. If it gets to be too much, just tell me and I'll back off immediately."

She bit her lip, his words making sense. She took a step back, leaning against the wall, needing a minute to let this all sink in. She *might* be able to do this—what he'd described. Minute by minute. No labels. No pressure. Friends at the core. Her deep need for him would be met. They could date. They could kiss. They could make love. She could sleep spooned against him. She could also leave in the middle of the night if she wanted. If she got scared and nervous at any time, she could retreat.

Right now, she felt more hopeful than scared. She could go with this. She didn't have to shut out what she needed. *Don't turn away this wonderful man. Try.* Like he did—like he was right now. "This sounds good to me, Diego, except for the part where I get everything I need and you're out in the cold."

His dark eyes sparkled with the in she'd given him. "In the cold? Are you kidding? You've come to mean so much to me that the iceberg in my chest completely melted. I'm warm all the time. I'm also Latino—hot-blooded." He smiled.

She couldn't help but laugh. "Can we really do this? Just as you said?"

He pulled her into his arms again. "I absolutely can. Because like I said, the core of us is friendship. And friends are there for each other no matter what. If I can kiss you, if I can make love to you, all the better, but I just want to be in your life. Yours and Robbie's."

"I like the sounds of that," she said, so touched by him that her eyes misted up all over again.

She was still worried, though—deep down and right on the surface—but if she could keep Diego Sanchez in her life in a way that didn't scare her every other minute, she was taking it.

Chapter Thirteen

Last night, when Diego had been saying goodbye to Jenna at the door, they'd discovered they both had today off. A rare, happy coincidence. He'd invited her and Robbie on an outing, hoping she'd say yes. He didn't want to overwhelm her with his presence, considering he'd stayed for a few hours.

After they'd come to an agreement on their relationship, Jenna had suggested they finally enjoy those delicious red velvet cupcakes he'd brought over for Robbie's seven-month birthday. They'd had their treats while watching a rom-com that had them commenting through the entire movie. They'd laughed and chatted, keeping the conversation light—about the film, funny stories from their childhoods, and what kind of dog they'd each get if their living situation ever got dog-friendly. Diego liked Great Danes and chihuahuas and wanted one of each. Jenna liked medium-sized, furry, smiley dogs, like Australian shepherds. They'd both agreed that lonely mutts at the shelter who needed homes would win their hearts and they'd want to take them all home.

And then it had gotten late fast. Diego had said he'd better hit the road since he didn't want to overstay his welcome so soon, and when Jenna didn't invite him to stick around longer, he wasn't disappointed. He'd truly meant all he'd said to her when he'd first arrived. Her terms. Her timeline.

And now, at 10:00 a.m., the three of them, Diego, Jenna and Robbie, were headed to the Tenacity Town Hall to see a special art show that Jenna had suggested. The show featured art from kids of all ages, from toddlers to teenagers. The daycare where Jenna worked had part of a wall devoted to their kids' work, including baby Robbie's artistic debut.

"We're here, Robbie!" Diego said as he turned into the parking lot. "I can't wait to see your handprints."

Jenna got out and unlatched Robbie's car seat, then snapped it into the stroller base. "Me too! I've seen it, of course, but not hanging on a wall! Robbie definitely liked having her hands plopped into the pink watercolor paint, didn't you, my little *artiste*?"

Diego smiled as he watched Jenna with her daughter. He'd never expected to be a dad, so he'd never pictured himself in the midst of something like this. As an uncle, sure. But this felt different because the tiny human having such an effect on him wasn't a relative who he adored simply because they were family. The intense protectiveness he felt for Robbie was brand-new to him.

As they headed toward the entrance, Diego was reminded of the Valentine's dance, Jenna in his arms and all the promise of that night—which had almost derailed. But things were back on track. He'd woken up feeling very positive about their talk last night. He'd been willing to go from zero to sixty because of how strongly he felt about Jenna, how much Robbie had come to mean to him, but he knew *he* should be going slowly for his own sake too. He hadn't let himself feel anything for a woman in seven years. And now he was spending the day with a single mom and her baby, a family of two who he'd do anything for.

This new plan of theirs was good for them both.

Inside, they waved and said hi to the few people milling around this early; the big crowd would come after school when the young artists came with their families. There was some serious talent among the children of Tenacity. Katie W., age 10, had sketched a drawing of a yellow Lab with such expression in the dog's face and eyes that Diego would have bought it were it for sale. A high school student painted her entire family with colored dots. Little Cowpokes Daycare Center had his favorite work, though. Various colored suns with long spokes around the orb, houses with no doors, lots of stick people. The art was beyond adorable.

"And the masterpiece," he said as they stopped in front of the pink watercolor. *Handprints by Robbie L, age 7 months.* "Great job, Robbie!" he said, bending down to shake her little hand.

Jenna grinned and took out a phone to snap a few photos of the artwork for her parents, then stepped to the side to text them.

He knelt down beside the stroller. "Love your use of shading, Robbie," he quipped, running a finger down the baby's soft cheek.

"Hey, Diego," said a male voice.

He turned to see a guy he'd gone to school with here in Tenacity. Linc Danvers, who'd been on the baseball team with him. A young kid was up on his shoulders, and his hands were on a stroller with a napping baby. Diego hadn't spoken to Linc since graduation. Tenacity was a small town, but there weren't many places to run into people. "Hey, Linc. Mini artist in the family?" he asked.

"Actually, no. My wife has a bad cold so I figured I'd get these two out of the house for a bit and this seemed like a fun activity. This big guy is Willis—he's four, and the baby is Sara. A year next month."

Diego smiled up at the cute blond boy, then peered into the stroller. "Happy almost birthday," he whispered to the napper just as Jenna came back over. "Linc, this is Jenna and the talented artist is Robbie. These are her handprints," he added, gesturing at the watercolor.

"Proud daddy," Linc said with a smile. "I know how that is."

Diego glanced at Jenna, whose expression tightened. "I'm actually a family friend," he said to Linc.

Linc nodded. "Ah. Well, nice to see you, Diego. And nice to meet you, Jenna. Enjoy the day."

As the guy headed down the hall, Diego was struck not only by what he'd said, but by the image of him walking with the little boy up on his shoulders as he pushed the stroller.

I actually do feel like a proud papa.

And I want to be wheeling Robbie about town. I want Robbie up on my shoulders, my hands around her ankles, someday.

And I want Jenna by my side.

He froze for a second at the realization that he was already quite serious about Jenna. It had happened without his awareness. Exactly like Julian had said it would.

"Cute kids," Jenna said kind of absently, her gaze on the next piece of art on the wall.

"Sorry about that." He had no doubt she'd know what he was referring to.

She was quiet for a second, then shook her head and touched his arm. "No worries, Diego. Really. I just reacted in the moment. You'd think I be used to it—Mike's been mistaken for Robbie's dad more than a few times the past seven months."

He smiled but there was a reason it didn't bother her until now, until Diego. Mike wasn't a love interest, a potential partner. Diego was.

"You have every right to feel protective of who her father is and his memory, Jenna."

She wrapped her arm around his and rested her head on his shoulder, surprising him. "You always understand me."

Because I love you, he thought out of the clear blue sky—and froze.

He did love her. *I love Jenna Lattimore.* He wanted to scream it down the hall, cupping his hand around his mouth like a megaphone.

If he could change to this degree, he had no doubt that with time and love and care, Jenna would fully welcome him into her and Robbie's life.

He was ready for it.

A couple of hours later, Jenna had just put Robbie down for her nap in the nursery when Diego came to the doorway. They'd had a great morning, enjoying the art show, then going for coffee and pie at the Silver Spur Café, something she rarely ever did given her strict budget. He'd insisted on treating—*I invited you out, so it's on me*. Then Robbie had started yawning so they'd brought her home. Diego had been about to leave when he said the squeaky bathroom door hinge was driving him nuts and it would take him two seconds to lubricate it. She'd jokingly mentioned she had a whole bunch of other little things that needed fixing, and he'd said he'd take care of it all and had gone to his pickup for his tool kit. She'd better watch out or he'd make himself a little too indispensable. Very nice and superhot was fine. But a man who could fix a leaky faucet was golden.

"Robbie asleep?" he asked, stepping inside to peer at the baby. "I love how she always naps with her arm crooked alongside her head, fist at her ear."

Jenna laughed. "My favorite thing is when she quirks her lip like Elvis." She gasped. "She just did it!"

Diego laughed too. "I have another invitation for you." He held up his phone. "Just got a text from my mom. Family dinner tonight. She's making her incredible enchiladas suizas and would love for you and Robbie to join us."

Surprise lit her face. "Really? That's so nice. Any particular reason or occasion?"

"Well, the whole family is invited because my sister Marisa and her husband, Dawson, are back from their honeymoon and everyone wants to see the photos. And I'll be honest about why *you're* likely invited—I was moping yesterday morning and I ran into my sister Nina and I might have told her I was worried about us. So she might have told my mom to add another plate at the table. Trying to do a little matchmaking, no doubt."

"Aww. We beat them to it."

He pulled her to him for a hug. "Yeah, we did."

She relished being in his arms. She'd been aware all morning that he'd been taking care not to overwhelm her. He'd been affectionate, but not overboard. And then there was the way he'd handled her reaction when his old school friend had mistaken him for Robbie's dad.

You have every right to feel protective of who her father is and his memory, Jenna.

They were taking their relationship minute by minute, and minute by minute Diego Sanchez was showing her that she'd been right about him all along.

"I'd love to go and meet your family. I'll put Robbie in her fanciest clothes."

He smiled. "I'll let my mom know," he said, sending a quick text back.

Over the next few hours, Diego took care of those issues around the house—the squeaky hinge, the leaky faucet, the bottom of a door that needed sanding, and since Jenna had wanted to move some furniture around, switching the desk and console table in the living room.

She looked around at the new arrangement and smiled. "I could not have managed that on my own. It's nice to have a brawny cowboy around."

He made a muscle with his arm and smiled. "So we'll leave in a half hour for my place."

They'd spent so much time together today, and with the exception of the art show and pie, they'd been right here, doing everyday things. In between his handyman fixes, he'd made a pot of coffee, looking like he belonged in her kitchen. And when he rooted around in the fridge to make some lunch suggestions—and then whipped them up sandwiches—she realized that he felt right at home and that it didn't make her feel funny. Instead, she felt...comforted. Excited.

"I'm really looking forward to meeting everyone," she said. "And to try those enchiladas. I'll just go get ready. Keep an ear for Robbie?"

"Will do," he said, dropping down on the sofa.

I trust you, she realized in amazement as she hurried to her bedroom to have this moment in private. She went to her dresser and stared at herself in the mirror, sure she must look different. Granted, she was just feet away from Robbie's nursery should Robbie suddenly start screeching out of control, but Diego had become a trusted person in her life the way Mike was.

And now she was meeting his whole family. Getting further enmeshed in his world. She knew she'd fall for this man fast and swift and hard no matter how slowly she tried to go.

One minute at a time, she reminded herself.

She freshened up her makeup and changed into dark jeans and her favorite emerald green sweater, adding gold earrings and a necklace to dress it up a little. When she came out of her bedroom, Diego had Robbie in his arms, swaying her back and forth by the patio door.

Singing her a lullaby that he clearly didn't know the words to and was adorably mangling.

She'd chuckle if she wasn't so touched. Did he know the way to her heart was through being this sweet and caring to her child?

"Forget our honeymoon pics," Marisa said as she oohed and ahhed over Robbie. "I could look at this precious baby all day."

They'd arrived a half hour ago, Diego getting more claps on the back and knowing looks in one five-minute period than he'd gotten in his entire life. Jenna had gotten a warm welcome, and everyone fussed over the baby. They were now seated at the dining room table, Robbie sitting in the playpen the Sanchezes had on hand for when Julian and Ruby visited with their little one. Little Jay was napping in his car seat, since he'd conked out in Julian's truck on the way over. Big sister Emery was sitting in her booster seat at the table with the grown-ups.

Diego's mother's gaze was soft on Robbie. "I'm always ready for grandchildren to fuss over," Nicole said. She didn't turn to look at Diego, but he felt as if she was—pointedly. Interestingly, he wasn't uncomfortable with the idea like he'd normally be.

"That goes triple for me," Will Sanchez said. His dad threw a grin his way. And instead of mock-coughing or changing the subject, Diego smiled back.

It was a lot easier being this new Diego.

"The more grandnieces and -nephews the better," Uncle Stanley added, wrapping his arm around his Winona, whose gaze was boring into Diego. As usual.

Trying to tell me something? he wanted to ask, but he knew better than to question the psychic. If she had something to say, she'd say it. And leave you to figure out what the heck she meant. All he knew for certain was that her pronouncements always came true.

Jenna sat beside Diego, answering Marisa's and Nina's barrage of questions about Robbie and what her favorite solid foods were so far and if she'd said her first word. He was aware of his relatives watching him—

them—and listening closely. How he looked at Jenna, how he spoke to her, how he handled Robbie.

"Must be serious," Luca had whispered when he, Diego and Julian had gone into the kitchen to refill the bowls of their uncle Stanley's homemade salsa for their mother's homemade tortilla chips—Diego's favorite on earth. "You brought not just Jenna but her *daughter*." His brother was studying him for the real answer just in case Diego wasn't forthcoming.

"I'm very serious about them both," he'd whispered back.

Both Luca's and Julian's eyes had opened wide in such surprise that Diego had to laugh. Hey, he got it. He'd been Tenacity's unofficial most confirmed bachelor for years.

Now, as they were enjoying the delicious enchiladas, the conversation moved to focus on a different Sanchez every few minutes. Marisa's wedding and the honeymoon, Julian's plans for the ranch he'd purchased, which he'd named The Start of a New Day Ranch, Ruby's report of Jay's well-baby checkup—all was very well—and Diego's mom's amazement that her home business as a seamstress had tripled profits from last month since so many folks had hired her to have their Valentine's Day date outfits taken in or let out. Nina, though, was on the quiet side and seemed distracted.

"Nina, any word on your search into the Deroy family?" Diego asked, sensing she had that on her mind.

Diego recalled that Nina had asked their uncle Stanley to use his newly discovered sleuthing skills to locate the Deroys—particularly Barrett, her first love. He hadn't been seen or heard from since he was sixteen, when he and his family suddenly left town. Why and what had become of them was a total mystery.

Nina's shoulders deflated. "I haven't been able to find out *anything* about them and neither has Uncle Stanley—not for lack of both of us trying. It's like Barrett vanished into thin air. I just want to know what happened all these years ago to make him and his family leave Tenacity. And where he is now. What he's doing."

Stanley looked at Nina. "I'm surprised that I haven't been able to find out anything. I left the online searches to you and know it didn't get you anywhere, but all my chatting folks up on my walks and trip to the grocery store were a letdown too. Sorry." He seemed lost in thought for a moment. "Nina, I do have to caution you that when the Deroys left town, they were persona non grata. Folks turned against them for some reason. I wonder if the family purposely destroyed any trail that could lead anyone to them."

Nina frowned. "I just wish I knew what happened back then. What did they do that was so terrible?"

Uncle Stanley threw up his hands. "I wasn't around back then and neither was Winona. But I think it might have had something to do with Tenacity itself and the town falling on hard times." He turned to Diego's parents. "Will, Nicole, do you remember anything?"

Nicole shook her head. "Will and I talked about it after Nina asked you to look into it all. We can't remember why they left. In fact, we're not sure anyone really knows. It was all a bit of a mystery."

Stanley nodded. "So this really requires a lot more digging on my part." He turned to Nina. "I promise you that I'm working on it."

Nina nodded. "I appreciate your help, Uncle Stanley. I just wish I knew why Barrett left town without saying anything to me. It just makes no sense. I don't get it."

"Maybe he found it too painful to say goodbye," Diego said, thinking about yesterday morning, how hard it was to leave Jenna's house knowing that it might be the last time he saw the Lattimores.

All eyes turned to him. The family definitely wasn't used to sensitive insight about matters of the heart coming from him.

"Maybe," Nina said with a nod. "That would make sense, I guess." Again, she seemed lost in thought.

"It is written in the stars," Winona suddenly said.

Now all eyes turned to the psychic at the table. Everyone was clearly trying to figure out what she meant. What, exactly, was written in the stars? And when? Nina hadn't seen Barrett in fifteen years.

"What do you mean, Winona?" Nina asked with so much angst in her voice that Diego knew this was really important to her. Finding Barrett. Getting to the truth.

"It's written in the stars," Winona repeated.

Written in the stars. Diego thought about the night in the guest room, when he and Jenna had stared out at the window at the stars and made their wishes.

His had come true. He'd tell her that sometime. When she needed to hear it.

If she needed to hear it.

"It's time to find answers," Winona added, and then sipped her wine. Her gaze bored into Nina's, then moved to Diego's.

Was she applying that to him too? At the moment, he didn't need any answers. He and Jenna were taking it slow, day by day, minute by minute. No labels, no pressure. He supposed he did have a burning question and maybe wise Winona knew it.

His question? If he'd be fully welcomed into Jenna and Robbie's life the way he hoped.

Chapter Fourteen

In the morning, Diego and his father were herding cattle into a farther pasture on the ranch, the bright sunshine warming up the cold temperature. He couldn't stop thinking about Jenna, wondering what she was doing right then. He knew she was at work at Little Cowpokes Daycare Center, maybe reading to the children in her group or leading an arts and craft activity. Maybe she was taking a break and visiting Robbie in the baby room, asking her daughter what she thought of the Sanchez family. He smiled at that. They'd both had a great time last night. He knew Jenna had because she'd said so and had clearly meant it—and had looked so happy and comfortable last night at his house. Chatting with his family, laughing, telling everyone about Robbie's latest milestones, talking about Bronco and how she'd just visited her parents there recently.

"She's lovely," Diego's mom had said right before they were leaving. "So warm and friendly—not to mention beautiful."

"A keeper," his dad had whispered when he and Diego had gone into the kitchen to get a second pie for dessert. The first had gone in minutes.

"Agreed," Diego had whispered back, and the happy look on his dad's face was something else. Diego had realized then that his parents had likely been really worried about him and his state of mind, and state of heart, the past seven years, the last few particularly after turning thirty, since he'd avoided commitment and love for far too long.

"Think you and Jenna will get married?" his father asked now, deftly directing his mare to herd the cattle to the left.

"I still can't believe that question can apply to me," Diego said, marveling at how much he'd changed. How much a woman and a baby had swooped into his heart and turned his life right-side up.

"Trust me, I know," Will said with a chuckle. "Your mom and I wondered if someone would ever crack open that stubborn heart of yours."

"Someone definitely did." He smiled, Jenna's beautiful face coming to mind. Her warm blue eyes, full pink-red lips that he'd kissed so passionately. Not in the last couple of days, but their night in the guest room would last him a while. There would be time for passionate kisses and much more when Jenna was ready. Right now, he was just glad she'd opened the door.

"You love her?" his dad asked, looking at his son intently.

Diego was once again in total wonder that such a question was being directed at him, the guy who never went on a fourth date.

"With all my heart," Diego said. "Robbie too. Crazy, right? What happened to me?"

His father laughed. "Love happened. I'm very happy it got you, Diego."

"Me too," he said. "I like it. Who knew?"

His father laughed again, but when a few of the cattle went a little rogue, the two cowboys stopped yakking and started herding.

A few hours later, when they were back at the barn with the horses, his dad said he'd make them lunch at the house if Diego was hungry yet.

But Diego had another idea for his lunch hour. Something that had been on his mind the past few hours ever since his father had asked if he thought he and Jenna would get married. If he loved Jenna.

Yes and yes.

Well, that first question relied on someone else and right now, marriage had to be the last thing on Jenna's mind.

But the second was all him and yes he did. Diego Sanchez loved Jenna Lattimore. Deeply. And he wanted to celebrate that. Quietly. Just by himself. It was a big deal and he knew it. And it needed a big gesture.

Which was why he found himself using his lunch hour to drive two towns over to where an online search had told him he'd find a nice jewelry store in Beaumont and Rossi's Fine Jewels. He wouldn't have the pick of the store, of course, but he'd find something just right and worthy of Jenna in his price range. He drove the half hour and parked in front, noticing a familiar blond and a tall, well-dressed man coming out of a restaurant across the street.

His ex. Caroline. She and the man got into a fancy SUV and drove off.

You'll never be more than just a cowboy on a middling ranch...

He waited a second to feel that old familiar twist in his gut, a rush of bitterness—something. But he felt nothing. A neutral nothing. It was as if he'd seen an old acquaintance whose name he could barely remember.

I'm over you, he realized. *Over the cruel things you said. I know who I am and what I have to offer. Jenna Lattimore taught me that.*

Damn, that felt good.

It's written in the stars. Winona Cobbs-Sanchez's words came rushing back to him. Maybe this was what she'd meant. That he'd come to this jewelry store. That he'd spot his ex. That it wouldn't affect him in the slightest. That all he'd have burning in his heart was his love for Jenna. And his very unexpected interest in buying her an engagement ring—which he had no intention of proposing with or giving her for a long time, of course—for two reasons. To symbolize how far he'd come and as tangible proof of his love for her, of his belief in them.

Proposing marriage to Jenna Lattimore was not an option—not yet. Diego might be ready for that major step, but she wasn't. He'd hold on to the ring for at least six months, maybe a year. Maybe two years. Jenna was his woman. And when she was ready, he'd know it. Then he'd get down on one knee and ask her and Robbie to spend the rest of their lives with him.

He walked into the shop and looked in the display cases, eyeing every ring. Nope, no, not remotely Jenna-like. Finally, there it was. Jenna's ring. The twinkling round diamond on a gold band inset with tiny diamonds was the one, just like she was.

It would set back his bank account, but he'd been saving for years. He had nine months of an emergency fund. He had a solid nest egg growing for retirement. Nothing to write home about yet at thirty-three, but he was getting there. He had a steady, solid paycheck. He could afford the ring.

He was a cowboy and proud of it. Being a cowboy had always given him the life he wanted, what he needed. It just took him a long time to realize that. If he hadn't met Jenna Lattimore, hadn't fallen for her, he might still be the same old Diego.

The new Diego had marriage on his mind. Very much so. If he had to wait another seven years to watch the woman he loved walk down the aisle to him, so be it. He'd wait.

Fifteen minutes later, the ring, engraved inside the band with *J, all my love, D*, was in a black satin box in his coat pocket.

Would wonders ever cease? He sure hoped not. Because it meant that someday, he would be married to Jenna and helping to raise the baby girl who'd sneaked inside his heart.

A half hour later, back at work out on the range on horseback, he'd stuck his hand in his coat pocket a few times just to feel the ring box there. To know. To celebrate all he felt for Jenna. At home later, he'd hide it in the back of his closet for safekeeping.

He had his hand in his pocket when he saw something furry and tall-eared suddenly dart out from behind the stand of evergreens about a hundred feet away. Horses didn't like sudden movements, and Dusty, one of his favorite mares, bristled.

Coyote.

It stared at Diego with its amber eyes, then darted to another stand of trees a lot closer to him.

Before Diego could even blink, the mare reacted, panicking and galloping hard with a sudden pivot. Diego was pitched forward hard—and that was the last thing he remembered.

Everything went black.

Jenna sat at a big round table at Little Cowpokes Daycare Center, leading the three- and four-year-old group in a fun self-portrait activity. The kids were having a blast. So was Jenna as she worked on her own drawing, coloring in her long tresses with a red crayon. She'd given her hair a little more bounce on the ends than it had, but hey, it was art.

She had an itch to draw Diego. She was no artist and she'd never capture his expression, let alone the shape of his eyes or nose or chin for that matter. She just couldn't stop thinking of him and how wonderful it had felt to be included in his family dinner last night. To be a part of all that love and conversation and good will. The Sanchezes were such a warm bunch, and there was no such thing as an empty plate or glass unless you were absolutely stuffed and couldn't eat another bite.

They'd both had to be at work early this morning, so by 10:00 p.m. last night she was in bed, thinking of Diego. How he'd deftly transferred a sleeping Robbie to her bassinet when he'd taken them home. How he'd pressed a kiss to the baby's forehead and just stared at her for a moment the way Jenna always did because sometimes she couldn't believe this wonder of a little human was hers. Diego had had that same look on his face.

Her head had been telling her one thing these past days. First to back away completely, then to take a baby step forward again. Extra slowly. But Diego was just too wonderful. Even with the family component, even with seeing Diego often, even with him holding her tightly, she could handle it. It wasn't too much. And it wasn't too little. Things were just right.

Last night, while she'd lain in the guest room bed to be reminded of her night with Diego, she'd thought for the first time that maybe in the future, maybe like a year from now, she could even see herself engaged to him.

She wasn't ready to call what they had *love*. That was too much. Much too much. But what they had was heartfelt and beautiful and filled her up.

As she gave her self-portrait some eyelashes, her phone vibrated in her back pocket. She pulled it out— an unfamiliar number. Ugh, probably spam. She ignored it. A minute later, her phone vibrated again to reveal a new voicemail.

"Back in two seconds," she said, stepping to the side of the table to listen to the message. "Keep coloring, kids!"

She pressed Play.

Jenna, it's Will Sanchez. I'm very sorry to leave this message but I know Diego would want you to know right away. I'll just say it plainly—his horse threw him this afternoon on the ranch. He's still unconscious and the hospital is running tests. We're at the Mason Springs Hospital ER, waiting and praying. Come as soon as you can.

Jenna's blood had run cold the moment she'd heard Will's voice, clogged with emotion, with worry and fear.

Oh God. No. No, no, no.

"Jenna?"

Was someone calling her name? She couldn't think, couldn't move. Her legs were shaking. Jenna was vaguely aware that Angela was at her side, saying, "Honey, what's wrong?"

Jenna finally looked at her boss, trying to find her voice. "It's Diego. His dad called. He got hurt. He's in the hospital in Mason Springs. It's thirty minutes from here." Her voice sounded both broken and robotic. She was going numb.

"Honey, you go do what you need to do," Angela said with a firm hand on Jenna's shoulder. "We'll keep Robbie here. If you're not back to get her by six, I'll take her home with me. No worries. Just go. Are you okay to drive?"

Jenna managed a nod and gave Angela a quick hug. "Thank you." A sob was rising up in her throat and she wanted to assure the kids—who were all staring at her—that she was all right. But she wasn't.

"Honey, go," Angela repeated. "I've got them. I've got Robbie."

Thank God for Angela.

Jenna hurried to the baby room for just a look at her daughter. Then she grabbed her coat and raced out.

She drove with two hands white-knuckled on the steering wheel the half hour to Mason Springs, two towns over from Tenacity.

She went slowly. Carefully. All she wanted was to get there.

Finally, she parked in the Emergency area and ran

inside. She saw the Sanchez family immediately, some sitting, some pacing, his sisters teary-eyed. She rushed over to the group.

"Will, thank you for calling me," Jenna said in a rush. "Please tell me he's okay." *Please, please, please.*

"We don't know anything yet," Will said gently. "They're running tests, and then the doctor will come talk to us. He's still not conscious."

Her knees were shaky and she felt unsteady, her hands trembling as she reached for the armrest before she dropped down on the chair.

"He has to be okay," she said into the air. "He has to be okay."

His mother, on the other side of her, reached for Jenna's hand and squeezed it, but Nicole Sanchez seemed too emotional to speak.

If he was unconscious, he'd been thrown *hard.*

What if…

No, no, no, no, she silently chanted over and over. *Please let him be okay.*

She grabbed her phone and quickly texted Mike: Diego in hospital.

He called her back right away, and she stepped into the vestibule. She barely managed to get out what happened.

"I'll go pick up Robbie from Little Cowpokes right now," he said. "I'll take care of her as long as you need."

She knew Robbie would be fine at the daycare, but Angela and Elaina had enough to do without babysitting for Jenna, kind as they were.

"I appreciate that, Mike. I'll check in later."

She disconnected and went back to the Sanchezes.

When one sat down, another got up to pace. Uncle Stanley and Winona both sat grim-faced, their arms entwined.

"Mr. and Mrs. Sanchez," said a woman in a white lab coat. Her face was unreadable. No assurance there whatsoever.

Everyone stood up. Including Jenna. Waiting.

"Diego is going to be okay," the doctor said. "He's awake and the scans are clear. He has a concussion and a nasty goose egg, and some bruising on his torso and legs. He'll have to keep to light activity for a week, depending on how he feels. No heavy lifting, mentally or physically. Not even a crossword puzzle for two weeks."

They all breathed a collective sigh of relief. There were hugs and crying. Nina was saying that she'd never seen Diego do a crossword puzzle in his life, so no worries there. That got a smile out of the group, and the mood changed from worry and fear to jubilation.

Diego was fine. He was okay.

Jenna wasn't, though.

Her heart rate was returning to normal, her mind was clearing, her hands stopping the constant trembling, but she wasn't okay.

She was aware of an awful numbness in her chest, a strange hollow feeling. She'd been absolutely right in the wee hours after she and Diego had slept together. When she'd known she couldn't possibly allow herself to love him. To date him. Be involved with him.

She could have lost Diego today. And she couldn't, wouldn't be able to take it. She knew that by how she'd reacted. The terror. Her heart pounding. Her legs shaking.

If something happened to Diego she'd be destroyed.

A wreck of a person, unable to function as she lay under the covers, not eating or sleeping.

Or being any kind of a mother to her baby.

Love meant loss. Harrowing loss. And Jenna had to be done with that. It wasn't better to have loved and lost. Jenna knew that.

She *hated* that saying.

The strangest sensation came over her just then. Like her heart shrinking. Closing in on itself. Robbie was in there, she thought numbly. With her family. And her memories.

There was no room left.

She had to say goodbye to Diego. Forever.

Chapter Fifteen

Diego had been cautioned not to think too hard because of the concussion. Good thing he didn't have to wonder why Jenna hadn't come to see him. He knew why.

He understood. He hated it, but he understood. Her worst fear about welcoming him into her life had come true for her.

Damn coyote.

He lay in his hospital bed, staring out at the overcast sky. That he was bruised and battered barely registered when his heart hurt like hell. The good news was that Dusty had escaped unscathed; the coyote must have slinked back into the woods. Dusty had made her way back to the ranch alone, which was how the foreman had known there was a problem. Diego had been lucky to be found so quickly.

He was stuck here overnight as a precaution, then he'd be sprung tomorrow if he could walk and talk well in the morning. He usually hated being in the hospital, but he still felt the remnants of the monster headache he'd awoken with, the over the counter extra-strength pain relievers thankfully doing their job.

Except for the ache in his chest, left side. That went deep and wouldn't be going away for a long time.

His whole family had come in, two at a time, which was the max allowed. The foreman and a couple of cowboys Diego was good buddies with had turned up with his favorite snack, a family-sized bag of Doritos. His dad had told him Jenna had been in the waiting room with them but had left after hearing from the doctor that he was all right.

He glanced at the annoying ticking analog clock on the wall. Vising hours were ending in twenty minutes. He longed to see Jenna's beautiful face, Robbie's bright blue eyes and wispy auburn curls. But he didn't expect Jenna to come. This whole experience had to be very rough on her. Ever since they'd had that conversation the day he thought she was dumping him, he'd actually taken notice of instances where he could be more careful. He'd stopped trying to get through a yellow light. He no longer jaywalked, even in sleepy Tenacity because you just never knew who was coming speeding from around the corner, who was backing out of a spot when you weren't paying attention. He'd taken greater safety measures when he'd been fixing the little things in her home—not just jumping down from the stepladder without a thought. He planned to avoid the open range during a thunderstorm, just in case lightning was looking for someone to strike.

But accidents happened. Period. Coyotes darted from woods and spooked horses.

Jenna knew that. It was why she wasn't here. Because any minute, any day, she could lose him. He'd been lucky today. He might not be tomorrow.

She wasn't coming. Ever.

Unless... He sat up a bit, his head not appreciating

that. Maybe Jenna had left because she was thinking things over and just needed some time. Maybe she'd realized that yes, accidents *did* happen and that shutting out love wouldn't be much help.

He felt himself brightening. Until he knew otherwise, he was going with that.

There was a tap on the door. "Diego? It's Jenna."

His heart gave a leap at the sound of her voice. It was as if his wishing, his positive thoughts, had conjured her. This had to be a sign—a good sign—that he was on the right track with his assumption. That she was coming to tell him that she loved him and wanted him by her side, that his accident made her realize that. He was 51 percent sure, anyway.

But the missing ring was definitely a *bad* omen. He'd asked the nurse for the contents of his coat pockets. They'd given him a set of keys and his wallet, which had been zipped in the left pocket. There'd been nothing in the right pocket, they'd said. Where the ring had been. The ring box he'd been touching when Dusty had reacted.

He'd confided in his Uncle Stanley about the ring. If the little black box had gotten thrown with him, it probably would have landed somewhere near him, but the foreman and the cowboy who'd gone to look for Diego when the mare had returned alone hadn't mentioned seeing anything.

Maybe the ring box fell in a critter hole. Or ended up under some brush in the tree line. The coyote could have grabbed it in its mouth and run off with it, hoping it was a snack.

Nope, coyote, it's just a symbol of what I hope is my

future. A forever love with the woman and baby I want to spend my life with.

Once he was healed up, he'd take a less easily spooked horse out to that area and look for it.

"Come on in," he called.

She came in tentatively, then rushed over to the bed, her hand on her heart. She seemed so flustered and emotional and wasn't saying anything.

"You should see the other guy," he said with a grin.

Not even a hint of a smile appeared on her too pale face.

"I'm okay, Jenna," he assured her. "Really. I am." The more he looked at her, the less sure he was of what she was going to say. "Where's Robbie? With Mike?"

She nodded, then let out a breath. "When your dad called and left me that message, I was so scared. And while I was in the waiting room, not sure if you would be all right—" She shook her head and stopped talking, dropping down on the chair beside the bed. "I'm so, so relieved that you're all right."

"I'm definitely all right," he said, reaching for her hand and holding it. "Just a headache. And I can't tax my brain for a solid week. Or do anything that might cause another concussion, like go about my daily life." *I could lay on your sofa and think about how much I love you. Hold Robbie and feed her spoonfuls of pureed sweet potatoes and little bites of scrambled eggs...*

She looked away for a moment, and the hope he'd felt just two minutes ago was dissipating. "Diego, I..." She got up and walked over to the window, staring out. "I wish I were a stronger person. I wish—" She looked down and wiped at her eyes, his heart breaking for her. *Oh, Jenna.* "I'm sorry," she said in a broken voice. "But—" The tears came then, and she covered her face with her hands.

"Sweetheart, it's okay," he said, a clump of sadness settling inside him. It wasn't okay, not for either of them, but he had to be gentle. He'd always known that. "Come sit next to me."

She sniffled and moved to the chair. He took her hand and just looked at their entwined fingers, the ache in his chest deepening, widening. What were the magic words? What could he say to make her stay in his life without pressuring her? He wouldn't do that. But he would tell her how he felt.

"Listen, Jenna. You're the best thing that's ever happened to me. You and Robbie. You changed my life. You changed *me*. You showed me that I do have something to offer. Myself." He took a breath, not sure anything he was saying could change things. "I love you, Jenna Lattimore. And like I said the day after we made love, I'm not going to try to pressure you. I love you too much for that. I want you in my life. But if that's not possible, then maybe it's a matter of time. I waited seven years to feel like this. I can wait another seven."

He had to pray that she just needed some time. To get over this awful experience. To get used to loving him. To accept that love couldn't be denied, no matter how scared you were of it.

He had to hope she'd come back.

Tears misted her blue eyes. "You're a dream man, Diego. Someone will snap you up by then," she said in an almost whisper, her voice cracking.

"Who can compare to you and Robbie?" he asked,

trying to get a smile on his face, but this hurt so damned badly that he couldn't. His voice had shaken on the baby's name.

"I care about you too much to be at all wishy-washy," she added. "I can't be with you. I can't live in this state of worrying twenty-four seven. Of being so afraid. I know it's weak. But it's where I am."

"Jenna, you're not weak. You're actually one of the strongest people I know."

He could list twenty reasons how and why that was true. But he said he wouldn't pressure her to look at things differently, so he'd leave it at that.

Diego had never been much of an optimist. But now? His hope was all he had. What he and Jenna had was pretty powerful. It might do the work for him. It might bring her back to him.

But right now, he had to let her go.

The wish he'd made on the star from the window in her guest room wouldn't be coming true for a long time. That they'd become a family. The three of them.

"Do something for me?" he asked.

"Sure," she said, a bit nervously.

"Text me the photo you took of Robbie's pink handprints."

Tears streamed down her cheeks. She managed a nod, squeezed his hand and then hurried out.

And his heart cracked in two so hard that he had to grab the weird buckwheat pillow his sister Marisa and Dawson had brought him and clutch it against his chest.

For the next week, Jenna had gone to work and then straight home. She'd tried very hard not to think of

Diego. Not to wonder how his concussion was faring, if his bruises were fading. She avoided the guest room, keeping the door closed against the memories inside.

As promised, she'd texted him the photo of Robbie's pink watercolor handprints, and it was the very bitter-sweet goodbye she'd needed. A final gesture. But that night, all she could think about as she'd lain in bed was Diego seeing a text from her, thinking that maybe she'd changed her mind about them, and then it just being the photo. She'd kept her word, nothing more. She could see him looking at the watercolor, wistful. Missing her and Robbie. The pieces of her shattered heart still managed to go out to him. *I'm sorry I hurt you, Diego. I know some wonderful people, and you are tops. You didn't de-serve that. Not when you came so far yourself.*

She hated that part. He'd changed because of her, *for* her. And she was running from him. For self-preservation.

It had been a rough week emotionally. She'd taken care of Robbie, she'd knitted hats and started a sweater for her mom's upcoming birthday, she'd made big batches of different soups to keep her distracted and eat-ing, she'd had visits from Mike, who'd come by or texted every day. Even her parents had come for an overnight when she'd confided in her mother—crying through most of it—that she'd broken her own heart by needing to end her relationship with Diego.

Her father had taken one look at his saddened daugh-ter and had pulled her into a hug, then said he was going to give it to her straight: She meant the world to him, he understood how she was feeling, but denying herself the man she loved wasn't the answer.

You love us, Jenna. Your mom and me. You love Rob-bie. You can't shut us out. You can't stop loving us out of fear that something will happen. So I don't think you should do that with Diego.

Steven, her mother had chastised her husband. *If you understand, then let Jenna feel what she feels.*

Her father had tightened his hug, comforting her with his support, even if he thought she was making a mistake.

Honesty is good, Jenna had said. *But I just can't, Dad. I can't.*

They'd made her tea and baked her cookies, doted on their grandbaby, and when they'd left the next morning she'd given some thought to what her father had said, made a little easier by her mom taking her "side." But there was a difference between her loving the people in her life and not shutting them out and doing that to Diego. He wasn't family, even if he felt like family. He hadn't been there all along. He was new.

And loving anyone new was out of the question. His accident had hit that home.

The doorbell rang. Maybe Mike or Angela, who'd stopped by a few days ago with a crock of her famed macaroni and cheese and a hug.

Jenna opened the door, surprised to find Stanley and Winona on her doorstep, bundled up in wool hats and parkas—Winona's in her trademark purple.

"I'm not much of a talker," Winona said, "but I have something to say to you."

Jenna almost jumped. Winona seemed serious. Jenna stepped back and welcomed them in, taking their coats and hats and hanging them up.

They accepted her offer of coffee, and the cookies she'd said her parents had baked the other day, and she brought a tray into the living room, where they sat on the sofa. She sat adjacent on the love seat, and they both turned toward her.

Winona's blue eyes bored into her. "You already love Diego so you might as well share your life with him. Why love him from a distance?"

She must have looked taken aback because Stanley suddenly said, "Diego didn't say a word to us. He must have confided in one of his siblings about why he seemed so miserable and word spread among the family so that we could try to cheer him up."

Jenna gave something of a nod, a little uncomfortable. But somehow comforted at the same time. Stanley and Winona had been a huge support to her at the Valentine's dance, and she'd never forget it.

She opened her mouth to try to explain why she had to send Diego out of her life, but it wasn't easy. "I just have to protect myself" was all she could manage.

"I know everyone's different, Jenna," Winona said. "But I'll tell you this. I've been through it all and then some. So has Stanley. But we're still here, living and loving because both are a blessing." Their wedding rings glinted in the afternoon sunlight coming from the windows. "That's all I wanted to say." She picked up her cup and drank, then took a cookie and sat back, staring straight ahead.

Jenna looked away for a moment, everything suddenly…jumbled.

Stanley cleared his throat. He suddenly looked a little nervous. Like he was debating whether or not to tell her something. "Jenna, I wasn't sure if I should do this or not, but... I feel it's right."

Okay, now *she* was nervous.

"Diego told me that when he got thrown," Stanley said, "there'd been something in his coat pocket that must have gotten thrown too. Took me a while, but I found it. I think you should know the story behind it."

Jenna tilted her head, wondering what it could be.

Stanley set a small black ring box on the coffee table and Jenna gasped, her eyes going wide. "I told Diego I found it and that I was surprised he'd buy a ring at this point. He explained that he had no intention of giving it to you for at least six months—that it was a symbol. Not just of how far he's come, but as tangible proof of his love and belief in the two of you."

Oh, Diego, she thought, deeply moved by *both* Sanchezes' intentions—Stanley at wanting her to know all this and Diego for the secret gesture.

"That's lovely," Winona said, nodding at her husband.

Stanley put his arm around his wife. "It is that. Jenna, he knew you weren't ready for a proposal. But he wanted to have it for when you were. I was about to leave it on his dresser in his room, but he asked me to hang on to it for him. Said I was lucky and he wasn't."

Jenna's eyes misted with tears. She stared at the little box.

The elderly couple stood. "We'll leave you be," Stanley said. "Thank you for the coffee and cookies. Oh— and rest assured that we won't breathe a word of our visit to Diego. We're meddling enough as it is, but sometimes..."

Jenna tried to manage a smile, but she was on the

verge of breaking down. Her heart was thudding, her legs felt shaky and her mind was spinning. But she did have one burning question. "Can you tell me how Diego's doing?"

"He's doing great," Stanley said. "Going a little stir-crazy, but we've all been watching him like hawks to make sure he doesn't do anything taxing."

Relief flooded through her. "I'm very glad to hear that."

She walked them to the door. Stanley gallantly helped his wife on with her coat, and Winona lovingly wrapped his red scarf around his neck.

Winona stared at Jenna, her blue eyes so intent on her that Jenna was almost mesmerized. "It's written in the stars. But you know that, dear."

Before Jenna could say anything—not that she had a thought in her head at the confusing, emotional moment—Winona put her arm around her husband's and they left.

Jenna dropped down on the little bench in the entryway, Stanley's words echoing in her head. *A symbol… of his love and belief in the two of you…*

She went back into the living room to collect their coffee cups and plates, eager to have some busywork to do so she wouldn't sit and ruminate on all Stanley and Winona had said and shown her. Their visit had been a lot. She was reaching for the cups when she gasped. Stanley had accidentally left the ring box on the coffee table.

She grabbed it and hurried to the door, but their car was already heading down the street.

Jenna bit her lip and closed the door slowly, then went back into the living room.

She sat down, setting the box back on the coffee table. *Open it*, she told herself. *Do that, at least.*

She took the box in her hands. She sucked in a breath, then lifted the lid, and tears misted her eyes again. A round diamond on a gold band with little diamonds all around it. Just beautiful. She could see that something was engraved inside the band.

She took the ring from the box and tilted it to read the engraving.

J, all my love, D.

As she sat there, closing her hand around the ring, a barrage of voices entered her head. Her father telling her that she couldn't stop loving them and Robbie out of fear that something would happen. That she shouldn't do the same with Diego. Mike, just that morning, saying that while he'd always feel overprotective of her, he liked Diego for her. *No, scratch that,* he'd said. *He* loved *Diego for her.* For her and Robbie.

Winona's words. *You already love Diego so you might as well share your life with him. Why love him from a distance?*

Stanley's: *He knew you're weren't ready for a proposal. But he wanted to have it for when you were.*

Diego's: *You're the best thing that's ever happened to me. You and Robbie. I love you, Jenna Lattimore.*

And her own now: *I can't love you.*

And a smaller voice, from very deep down saying, *But I do.*

Winona's voice again, echoing: *Living and loving are a blessing.*

Yes, they were. She and Robbie were here. She knew what Rob Lattimore would want for them both. Happiness. Love. Support. Big strong arms that he could no longer wrap around them.

She *knew* it.

She froze, then her gaze shot to the stairs. She pictured Robbie sleeping in her bassinet, little fist by her ear. Lips making an Elvis quirk. What was she teaching Robbie about the blessings of life and love? To run from both the way she was doing now?

She bit her lip and sat there for a while, just thinking, looking at the photos on the mantel. Her as a new mother holding her baby, wanting to give her the world the same way that Diego wanted to give *them* the world.

Finally, she put the ring box in the pocket of her cardigan and went upstairs to check on her daughter. To *be* with her daughter was more like it.

No. To tell her something. Something she didn't understand or even think about until just now.

Her daughter was still fast asleep, her fist indeed up by her ear in the way that made Diego smile. Jenna's heart could burst any second it was so full.

"Robbie," she whispered. "I forgot something in all this. And it's about you and what I want you to know. What I want for you. If something terrible happens to someone you love, if you lose someone, I wouldn't want you to hide yourself away. I'd want you to see life and love as the blessings they are, like Winona said. Love is everything. It's *everything*, Robbie. And I need to show you that I'm strong like Diego said I was."

Robbie Lattimore opened her eyes. Jenna gasped in surprise. A sign, for sure.

So what are you going to do about it? she asked herself, putting the beautiful ring back in the box.

Chapter Sixteen

Diego was making himself as useful around the house as he could. That primarily meant cooking, since he discovered he actually liked whipping up meals and there were three occasions to do it during the day at standard times, providing some much-needed structure. Over the past week, he'd made omelets stuffed with all kinds of interesting fillings and cheeses for breakfasts, piled-high sandwiches for lunch, and broiled steaks and baked chicken and even made his own pasta for dinners. Uncle Stanley had said it wasn't half bad, either.

Right now, an overcast Thursday afternoon, he'd just added the hominy and red chiles to his attempt at *pozole*, a beloved Mexican soup that was a favorite of Uncle Stanley's. Stanley had been a godsend the past week and deserved a special treat. Not bringing up Jenna when it was obvious Diego didn't want to talk about her, but plopping down next to his grandnephew in the living room to watch a game or movie or laugh over Bugs Bunny arguing with Elmer Fudd. The *pozole* was Diego's way of saying thank you *and* needing to kill a good couple of hours.

The kitchen smelled amazing. He had the house to

himself, so there was no one to appreciate the fragrant aroma emanating from the big pot every time he took off the lid to stir the soup. His father was out on the range, his mother was delivering garments she'd worked on and Luca was working.

He'd had lots of time to think about Jenna this past week. Their last conversation. The two nights they'd spent together, one very passionately. Her beautiful face.

And Robbie too. He missed that baby so much. A couple of times he'd even opened the text with the handprint photo, just to feel connected to her.

Every day he wanted to get in his pickup and drive to Jenna's house. And every day he stopped himself. He had to let her come to him. He just wasn't sure she ever would.

He heard a car pulling up and went to the window. Finally, someone to appreciate his delicious smelling *pozole* and be his taste tester. He pulled aside the curtain to see who it was.

Whoa.

Jenna.

He went to the front door and opened it. Jenna was coming up the path, carrying Robbie in her car seat. He grabbed his jacket because it was freezing and met her on the porch. "Is everything okay? Is Robbie okay?"

She smiled and turned the car seat around so he could see Robbie's face. She was sleeping. "We're okay. I just wanted to come see you. Tell you something."

Maybe she was leaving town. Selling her house and moving back to Bronco to be near her parents. He was glad for them but sad for himself. Out of sight often meant out of mind. If and when she was ever ready to love again, she'd have forgotten all about him.

They came inside and he closed the door behind her, taking her coat. She unsnapped Robbie's fleece bunting, then picked up the seat.

"Follow me to the kitchen," he said. "I spent so much time on tonight's dinner that if it burns I honestly might cry."

And he'd done his share of crying earlier this week, not that he liked to admit it. In the shower. In bed at night. He'd stopped, the sadness so close to the surface moving down deeper, where it hurt even worse.

She sniffed the air. "Mmm, something smells amazing."

"Mexican soup called *pozole*. That's what I do these days. Cook. And start uninteresting conversations about whether tomatoes are a fruit or a vegetable. Did you know that cast iron pans are best for getting a good sear on a steak if it's too cold to grill outside? This is what happens to a cowboy with a lot of time on his hands. He starts googling."

She was looking at him with sort of a happy expression on her face. Not like a woman who'd come to tell him that she was leaving Tenacity. Or that they'd never see each other again.

"What did you want to tell me?" he asked, needing to hear it, get it over with.

She gently set the car seat down. "That I love you, Diego. I think you know that already, given that I was so scared I had to cut you out of my life. But I want to say it. I love you. So much."

He almost gasped. "You love me," he repeated, letting her words sink in.

"I had some help coming to a few important realizations. My father gave it to me straight, as always. Mike. And Stanley and Winona—just a couple of hours ago."

He mock-narrowed his eyes. "What did they have to say?"

"Winona reminded me that life and love are blessings. Sounds like something a person hears every day and already knows. But her words hit me hard. I'm not one to mess with blessings, Diego. I understand now that I'm always going to be nervous about bad weather and spooked horses and rickety ladders. Life is all about risks. But love is the greatest reward. That's what I want to teach Robbie. When I realized that, I understood. I finally understood."

Wonders *would* never cease. He was sure of that now. "You have no idea how happy you're making me."

"Good. Because I know I made this week even harder on you than it started out." She reached into the pocket of her thick black sweater and pulled something out.

The ring box.

He gaped at it, feeling his cheeks burn. "Um, first of all, how did you get that?" he asked, then his eyed narrowed again. "Stanley." He shook his head with a smile. "You're not supposed to have that for like seven years."

Jenna laughed. "Stanley told me the story of this ring. And he left it with me—supposedly accidentally."

"I know you're nowhere near ready for a proposal and a ring, Jenna." He held out his hand to take back the box. "I gave it to Stanley for safekeeping, but I feel so lucky now that I'm ready to hold on to it for when you are."

But instead of giving him the box, Jenna moved it close to her chest. "Actually, I thought maybe you'd slide the ring on my finger."

Now he did gasp. "What are you saying?"

"I'm saying I'm ready to have you in my life, full throttle. I'm ready to love you with all my heart. I'm ready."

Diego was so floored that he was grateful to get down on one knee because his legs were shaking. "Jenna Lattimore, love of my life, will you marry me?"

Tears sprang to her eyes—happy emotional tears, this time. "Yes. I will."

He stood and slid the ring on her finger, the diamond sparkling in the kitchen. "I promise to be the husband you deserve and the father figure Robbie needs. I promise to give you everything I am."

He wrapped her in a hug and kissed her.

"I don't want to protect myself from the man who makes me feel safest," she whispered. "And very loved."

He kissed her again, his heart thudding. "You know, I told Stanley he should hold on to that ring because he was lucky and I wasn't, and I'd probably end up losing it again somehow. But I'm the luckiest man in Tenacity. In Montana. Maybe the world. Because I'm going to marry you and help you raise Robbie. I love you both so much."

She leaned up to kiss him. "We love you back."

"No rush on planning the wedding, Jenna. We can wait a couple of years. As long as I know you're mine, I'm good. My wish on that star came true, after all."

She smiled and kissed him again. "Actually, I was thinking how cute it would be to have Robbie walk down the aisle at our wedding. Toddle down, really. That's just four, five months away. I can be a June bride."

His heart was overflowing. "I'm very happy to hear that. I guess the Sanchez kitchen wasn't the most romantic place to get engaged. Sorry about that."

Jenna laughed. "I loved every second of that *pozole*-scented proposal, and I'll never forget it."

He tightened his arms around his fiancée and held her tight, then kissed her with all the passion he'd held back this past week.

Diego thought back to the after-party in the Tenacity Social Club, the night he saw Jenna for the first time. Saw Robbie in her yellow snowsuit. His two great loves.

He couldn't wait to tell his *tio* that he had an answer to his question about which Sanchez would be the next to get married.

Turned out that Diego might not be the next Sanchez getting married, after all.

Because a week ago, the day after Diego was cleared by his doctor to resume normal activities—happily earlier than expected—another Sanchez had a big surprise.

Julian had proposed to Ruby—on Valentine's Day!

The eldest Sanchez sibling and his bride-to-be had wanted to keep their engagement to themselves for a bit, particularly to let four-year-old Emery get used to the idea and for Julian, Ruby, Emery, and baby Jay to just revel in the fact that they'd truly be a family soon. And when Diego had gotten hurt, they'd held onto the news for a while longer.

Now, the Sanchez family was gathered in the dining

room at their home for a special dinner—to celebrate the two engagements.

Not only were Ruby's two little ones officially joining the family, but so was Robbie Lattimore.

The whole family had helped with this particular meal—everyone's favorite tacos, which meant every possible type of filling from carnitas to chicken to guacamole, and every type of topping.

Diego had just finished ribbing Julian about how he was on his third taco when they'd just all sat down five minutes ago. Beside Julian was Ruby with her twinkling engagement ring and baby Jay, and four-year-old Emery. Across the table were Nina and Luca, and Marisa and Dawson, and Diego sat next to Jenna, with Robbie in her highchair on her other side. The Sanchez *madre* and *padre*, Nicole and Will, were on Nina's other side.

"I have to ask this again?" *Tio* Stanley said with a grin, passing the big platter of the soft tortillas he'd made to Diego, who sat beside him.

Jenna took a sip of her sangria, also made by Stanley with his bride Winona's help. "Ask what?"

Stanley's brown eyes sparkled. "Which Sanchez is next to get hitched, as you say here in Montana."

Diego laughed. "Who knows? Maybe it'll be Luca. Maybe he'll beat us all to the altar." Luca was probably the most easygoing of the Sanchez siblings, but the bachelor cowboy wasn't even dating anyone.

Luca's gaze shot up. "Hey, find me the right woman, and who knows?" Ha. Like Diego said, easy-going. What a difference between the two of them. But hey, stubborn Diego had gotten where he'd needed to be. Right here with Jenna and Robbie.

Diego glanced at his sister Nina, sitting across the table. Nina was pushing rice around on her plate—and not saying much. She had a pleasant enough expression plastered on her face, but Diego had a feeling she was thinking about the guy who got away. Her old teenage love, Barrett. Now was not the time to tease her.

"Maybe we'll have the first ever Sanchez family double wedding!" *Tio* Stanley said, raising his glass of Sangria.

"Maybe we just will," his psychic bride, Winona, said.

What Winona Cobbs-Sanchez said was nearly always the case, whether in a week or a year, so they all figured there would be a very big family celebration in the coming months.

"I think Robbie wants to try a very tiny taco bite," Jenna said, "now that she's part of this big, wonderful clan, she'll get to try lots of Mexican specialties."

Diego got up and knelt down beside the adorable baby girl he loved so much, the child he would raise as his own, though he and Jenna would keep the memory of her birth father alive in her heart.

As his fiancée smiled at him, he took a small piece of tortilla and filled it with a tiny bit of shredded carnitas, a sprinkle of cheese, and held it front of the baby's mouth. "Try this, Robbie!"

The little lips parted and she took the bite.

Her blue eyes widened and twinkled and she opened up again.

"She loves tacos!" Diego said, grinning. "She wants more!"

Jenna laughed. "I love being part of this family."

For the next forty-five minutes, they ate, talked, laughed and made all kinds of wedding plans, from the outrageous to the simple. Stanley was saying something about a marching band down Central Avenue.

All Diego cared about was marrying the woman he loved, taking good care of little Robbie, and making good on his promise to be the man, husband and father this family deserved forever.

* * * * *

Don't miss the next installment of the new continuity
Montana Mavericks: The Tenacity Social Club
A Maverick's Road Home
by USA Today *bestselling author Catherine Mann*
On sale March 2025
Wherever Harlequin books and ebooks are sold.